CHELSEA'S CHOICE

THE RECLUSIVE MAN

KATHLEEN LAWLESS

Chelsea's Choice is a work of fiction. Names, characters, places, and incidents are either the product of the author's imagination or are used fictitiously, and any resemblance to actual persons living or dead, business establishments, events, or locales, is entirely coincidental.

Cover design by NE Fraser

ISBN print: 978-1-989873-43-4

Dedicated to my own real-life hero who is always so generous with his love and support.

CHAPTER 1

Chelsea pumped the pedals of her shiny new bicycle as she made her way slowly down the main street of Bullet, swerving to avoid horses, carriages and the assortment of pedestrians, all ages who stopped, mouths agape, to stare. She must look a sight, as she had yet to quite get the hang of this thing. It turned out staying upright while balancing on two wheels was a lot harder than the fellow back East had made it look.

Up ahead, she spotted the sign for the hotel and carefully slowed the bicycle. When she reached her destination, she stopped and dismounted as gracefully as possible. For the sake of decorum while traveling across the country by train, she'd worn a full skirt that ended just above the ankle, sadly missing the freedom of her cycling bloomers, which she had purchased with ease of riding in mind.

She leaned the bicycle against the hotel's front wall near the door and straightened her hat before she rushed excitedly into the lobby. She spun in a circle, hardly able to believe she was really here! The hotel's interior was grander than she'd pictured as she listened to her cousin's enthusiasm for the project, to build and manage the town's first hotel. The oversize, high-ceiling room boasted a piano in one corner, a colorful carpet covering a good portion of the shiny wooden floor, and several large vases of exotic blooms tastefully arranged on various tabletops.

Since her boots were less than pristine she stuck to the wood, their heels against the floor announcing her arrival long before she reached the desk.

"May I—" Standing behind the desk, Henrietta looked up and bit off her words. In a single move she rounded the massive piece of furniture and rushed toward Chelsea. "Am I seeing things?"

"I'm very solidly real, Cousin." Chelsea hugged Henrietta, happy laughter bubbling in her throat.

"Last time I was home you threatened to come for a visit one day, but I never expected—"

"That I'd actually make good on my word?" Her grin widened. "Surprise!"

"You should have let me know. I would have met the train."

"You're a busy woman. I didn't want to impose. Besides, it was one exciting adventure after another, making my own way here."

"You must stay at the ranch while you're here," Henny said, looking around. "Where are your things?"

"In town at the stage coach depot. I was hoping you could send that handsome husband of yours to fetch them."

"Braydon's rarely here. Affairs at the ranch keep him busy."

"So, he really is a cowboy." Chelsea glanced around in approval. "And you run this place all on your own. You are my inspiration!"

"Hardly on my own. Georgina is here helping most of the time, plus I have a most capable staff."

Chelsea continued to admire the spacious, tastefully-appointed room. "It's amazing, seeing first hand your dream come to life! I remember you talking about it when you were home on your honeymoon."

"I didn't do it on my own," Henrietta said. "How long will you be in Bullet? I'm dying for you to meet the family."

"Indefinitely," Chelsea said happily.

"Indefinitely?" Henrietta's smile faded. "Seriously?"

Chelsea nodded and slung her arm around Henrietta's shoulder. "You, dear cousin, are my inspiration. I remember the family members being so negative when you left Argentina, only to eat their words years later when you returned with your handsome husband in tow and countless tales of your treasure-hunting adventures."

"Luckily Papa and my brothers took to Braydon immediately, which helped soften their disapproval towards my actions," Henrietta said.

"Precisely why I left! I couldn't stomach turning into my mother, my life revolving around the men. I told everyone, 'If Henrietta can make her own way in the New World, so can I'." She cleared her throat. "I appreciate your offer to stay at the ranch, but I'd prefer to stay in town."

"As you wish. I'll have someone fetch your things from the depot. Will you be needing a horse and carriage?"

Chelsea shook her head. "I brought my own transport. Come see."

Reece stopped his wagon outside the hotel, his eyes narrowed as he stared at the bicycle propped against the front wall, looking totally out of place. Before he landed here, he'd seen a few of the two-wheeled contraptions in other parts of the country, but this was the first one he'd seen in these parts.

As he prepared to get out, Henrietta came through the front door, followed by a dark-haired woman who could have been her sister. Henrietta spotted him, and after a quick word to her companion walked over to the wagon, leaving the other woman staring his way in curiosity.

Reece hated folks staring at him, and pulled the brim of his hat down lower. "G'day, Henrietta. Taking a load to the train station in Yuma, so thought I'd stop by here first to see if you need any fresh blooms."

"The ones you brought last time are lasting beautifully, Reece. I tried what you suggested, adding a few drops of bleach and a pinch of sugar to the water."

"Good." In spite of himself, he inclined his head toward the other woman. "Kin of yours?"

"Yes, Chelsea just arrived. I came out to see the latest invention, her bicycle."

Reece made a face. "Don't see it taking the place of horseback, myself."

Henrietta raised her brow in a way he took to mean Chelsea was somewhat of a handful. "Reece, would you mind doing me a favor? When you get back from Yuma, could you please swing by the stagecoach depot? Chelsea left her things there and I don't have anyone here right now that I can send for them."

Reece grunted his assent. He'd do anything for Henrietta and the other Masons, who had respected his anonymity when he first got here and convinced the others in town to honor his request for privacy. Shame it also meant helping out that woman who even now was watching him with a calculating look in her eye. Worse yet, she appeared to be intent on joining them. He picked up the reins, anxious to be on his way without appearing rude, but before he could signal the horses Henrietta had started introductions.

"Reece, this is my cousin Chelsea. Chelsea, Reece has graciously agreed to fetch your things from the depot on his way back."

"That's so kind of you, Mr.—"

"Rawlings," he said gruffly.

"Look at the flowers," she squealed, raising up on tiptoe and peering past him into the back of the wagon. "I've not seen anything like it since I arrived in the Americas." Her English was perfect, underscored with a husky Latin American accent that stirred the hair on the back of his neck.

"Reece is a talented horticulturist," Henrietta said.

"I can see that." Chelsea subjected him to a calculating look. "Which only arouses one's curiosity as to his other talents."

Reece heard Henrietta's sharply indrawn breath and tightened his grip on the reins as he signaled to the horses. He drove away, conscious of those dancing dark eyes boring into his back. What was the world coming to? A woman speaking so freely to a stranger. Showing up here with a bicycle. A woman like that meant sure-fire trouble. Good thing he kept to himself.

"WHAT'S HIS STORY?" Chelsea asked, staring after Reece as he drove away.

"He arrived a few years ago, at which time he moved onto a small farm on the outskirts of town. All I know is that he was injured when the British troops invaded Perak years earlier. For some reason he never went back to Britain."

"A soldier," Chelsea said. "That explains the sad, lost look in his eyes. Like a man in exile."

"I think you're overdramatizing the situation," Henrietta said. "The man just wants to be left alone."

"You don't find it odd that he wound up here?"

"Not really. He and my friend Percy met up somewhere years back, then lost touch for a long time."

"Isn't Percy your mentor? The reason you came here in the first place?"

Henrietta's face softened. "Percy certainly gets credit for us venturing to this place that ultimately turned into a final destination for both of us."

"So now Percy and Reece hang out together all the time?"

Henrietta shook her head. "Percy's married. And Reece—"

"Reece what?"

"He keeps to himself. He never mentions his people back in England. Of course, neither does Percy. You'll find that with a lot of the settlers. They came here to get away and start fresh."

"Or perhaps to hide," Chelsea mused more to herself. "How did he come to be in the flower business?"

"That's my doing," Henrietta said, "although he probably rues the day I set foot on his homestead. I visited several smaller farms in the area, looking for someone who was willing to build a hothouse to grow exotic flowers and fruit locally. Reece was my last chance, and I was desperate enough to capitalize on our mutual friendship with Percy. Reluctantly he agreed to give it a go. As it turned out he has a real gift."

"He must enjoy it," Chelsea said.

"He told me once the flowers are the only company he needs. They listen to him ramble and don't talk back."

"Somehow, he doesn't strike me as one to ramble. More of the strong, silent type."

Henrietta sent her a look. "Don't get any romantic fixations while you're here."

"Why not?" Chelsea said cheekily. "It worked for you."

Henrietta laughed. "Did you hear how Braydon and I met? He made a most ungentlemanly wager with his brothers. Except I found out, deftly turned the tables, and made him look a fool. I never expected he'd forgive me, even though it served him right."

Chelsea noted her cousin's self-satisfied smile as she recounted the tale.

"As they say, all's well that ends well!"

"Yes well, neither Braydon nor I made things easy on the other."

"Precisely why you're my inspiration. I want the highs and lows of falling in love. The suffering and the joy."

"I don't think you can go looking for love, Chels. I believe it has to find you, often at the most inconvenient of times."

Henrietta's words only solidified Chelsea's determination to take charge of her own destiny.

AT YUMA's bustling train depot as Reece oversaw the loading of his precious blooms into the refrigerated railway car, he wondered what the porters would think if they knew he was the one who'd initially heard about the cold storage concept and invested heavily in those early day trials. As opportunities out West drew more settlers to ranching and farming, and newcomers from Europe continued to arrive on the East coast, Reece knew a surefire way to move perishables like meat and eggs across the country would be in high demand. At the time, he'd had no idea that his investment would ultimately benefit his growing and selling exotic florals. Or that there would be such a demand.

He was almost home before he remembered his promise to Henrietta to fetch her cousin's things from the stagecoach depot to the hotel. Reluctantly he turned the wagon around, hoping he could accomplish the task without running into Henrietta or her cousin.

Inside the depot, his jaw dropped when the clerk pointed to a huge pile of luggage against one wall. Three steamer trunks were stacked next to several other pieces along with two bulging valises. That wretched woman had traveled here with all this and a bicycle?

"'Bout time somebody got this lot outta here," the clerk said. "Can barely move, stuff's taking up so much room. The owner had to hire a separate coach just to transport it all."

Reece resisted the urge to mention how a well-placed, lit match would have taken care of the problem, and was sweating by the time he had everything situated into the back of the wagon. It took several lengths of rope to secure the load, and judging by the stares from passersby he made a comical sight driving from one end of town to the other.

He hated when people stared. Bad enough when someone tried to start up a conversation on one of his rare visits to town. Things had only gotten worse, thanks to Henrietta and her enthusiasm for greenhouse growing. He didn't dare tell her he was building a second one and had stopped haying all together because he just didn't have the time.

The propagation of his precious flowers was a lot more rewarding than growing hay, and judging by the enthusiastic response to his earlier efforts, the colorful blooms brought pleasure to lots of folks. Still, it was a shame people couldn't stick to their own business.

That blasted woman must have been waiting for him, for she pranced out the hotel's front door and scampered toward the wagon like a youngster on Christmas morning, actually clapping her hands together. "Thank you, thank you so much."

Reece grunted as he undid the ropes holding the lot in place.

She approached the back of the wagon and grabbed the closest valise, huffing with exertion as she set it down near her feet. Followed by the second. He was reluctantly going around the wagon to lend a hand, he had after all been raised a gentleman, just as she reached for the handle of a steamer trunk. When the trunk didn't budge, the expression on her face was almost comical. Looking his way, she sent him a sunny smile that did nothing to improve his disposition.

"I did get carried away, didn't I?

Before he could respond, he saw Henrietta's sister-in-law Georgina, and her husband Ben, the sheriff, walking toward the hotel.

"What all do you have there?" Ben asked companionably.

Reece blew out a breath. So much for getting in and out of town without drawing attention to himself. "Henrietta asked me to bring this young lady's things."

Georgina and Benjamin eyed the newcomer with undisguised interest. "I'm Henrietta's cousin, Chelsea," she said. "I'll be staying at the hotel."

"Short visit?" Ben said drily.

"Hardly." Chelsea giggled. "I told Henny I'm taking a leaf out of her book and never going back."

Ben gave his wife a peck on the cheek. "You better get back to work, love. I'll help Reece haul these things inside." He looked at Chelsea. "Staying at the hotel, I take it?"

"Henny invited me to stay at the ranch," she said. "But I'm keen to make my own way. Not dependent on anyone else."

Ben guffawed. "I suggest next time you don't pack more than you can carry by yourself."

Chelsea sobered. "I thought—I assumed there would be porters and man servants available."

"Might have been where you come from. Around here, people learn to do for themselves."

"I'll remember that," Chelsea said seriously. "I have a lot to learn about life in the West and I'm keen to experience everything the area has to offer."

Ben and Reece exchanged a look as they started moving Chelsea's things inside. As Georgina hustled Chelsea inside ahead of her, Reece heard her introduce herself and explain that she worked at the hotel with Henrietta.

"Nice of you to help out," Ben said, once they had the trunks stacked inside Chelsea's room, which was luckily on the main floor at the back of the hotel.

"Not much I wouldn't do for you and your kin," Reece said, taking off his hat and swiping a forearm across his brow.

"The wives worry you don't eat enough all on your own out there. That's why they keep inviting you to the ranch to share a meal."

"Maybe one day," Reece said. *The same day Hades froze*

over. Getting close to people meant revealing bits and pieces of the past that were better left alone.

"Just warning you. They aim to wear you down, figuring if they ask you often enough, you'll get tired of saying no."

"Wish they'd take on a different project," Reece said.

"Hey! You make a point of helping folks, it's only natural they feel inclined to reciprocate."

Reece didn't bother to respond, just climbed back in the wagon, gave Ben a wave and drove off.

CHAPTER 2

Hearing someone knock, Chelsea opened the door to her hotel room. Henrietta stood on the other side carrying a tray set for tea, which she put on the night stand, the only reasonably clear area. "I thought I'd come and see how you're settling in."

Chelsea moved the valises stacked on her bed out of the way, and cleared off the room's only chair. "I feel like such a ninny," she said. "The entire town must be laughing at me behind my back."

"People here tend to be kinder than that," Henny said. "Can I pour you a cup?"

Chelsea nodded. "I thought I was being so smart to bring everything I might need now or in the foreseeable future. Instead—" she waved a fluttery hand to encompass the room and its shambles. "The porters were horrified at every stop where I had to change trains. I had to hire a second stagecoach just to carry my belongings here from the end of the line in Yuma."

"For now, I suggest you hang onto a few things that are absolutely necessary. Pack up the rest. I'll have Braydon and some of his brothers find a spot on the ranch to store everything."

Chelsea blew out a breath. "I'm putting everyone out."

"You meant well," Henrietta said stirring her tea. "It's just a pity you didn't discuss your plans when Braydon and I were home. I could have given you some pointers about what to expect from life in a small Western town."

"The idea didn't strike me until you'd left," Chelsea said. "Even then it took several years to bring to fruition."

"Well, now that you're here, what *are* your plans?"

"I received an introduction to an editor at *Lipcott's Magazine.* I've sent him a few short stories and a piece about travel. He's interested in my writing. Specifically, life in the West from a city woman's perspective."

"Chelsea, you didn't exactly grow up in the city," Henrietta said kindly.

"I've spent time in several large cities these past years," Chelsea said stiffly. "I can do this."

"Well, I wish you luck," Henrietta rose.

"Wait," Chelsea said. "I was hoping you'd help me. Introduce me to some of the local ladies so I can hear their stories."

"People in small towns are naturally guarded against outsiders," Henrietta said. "Don't be surprised if you have difficulty getting anyone to talk to you."

"What about the ladies married to your husband's brothers?"

"I can guarantee most of them won't want to see their stories publicized or even fictionalized."

"Is that because they're hiding something?"

"No, Chelsea. They're just very private people."

Chelsea jumped to her feet. "But what about women helping women? I remember you telling us about one of the ladies who not only encourages others, she loans them capital when they need it."

"Laura's arrangements are private, not something to be spread across the pages of a periodical. Can you imagine how many charlatans would make their way here if they thought they could get money from her simply by asking?"

Chelsea narrowed her gaze. "How about your tales when you and Percy were hunting for lost treasure?"

Henrietta made a face. "Definitely not. No one would thank you if suddenly Bullet was invaded by a bunch of fortune hunters."

"I have to do something with my time, now that I'm here. I might as well have stayed home if my only options are to get married and settle down."

"Perhaps you should have thought of that earlier."

Chelsea stared thoughtfully at her tea cup as she stirred in milk and sugar. *Bicycling World* was a new periodical she'd recently come across. Perhaps something more specialized ought to be her target. She blew on her tea before she took a sip. Then there was her other idea.

AFTER SPENDING a few days exploring her new town, Chelsea's restlessness grew. Her entire focus till now had been making her way here, so now what? Henrietta hadn't exaggerated how close-mouthed the locals were. At first she'd introduced herself as a journalist. When that didn't prove useful, she changed tactics to act the part of an interested newcomer. Unfortunately, by that time word of her inordinate interest in the town and its inhabitants had already spread far and wide, to the point she found it nearly impossible to engage anyone in conversation.

The postmaster gave her a suspicious look when she asked for directions to the Rawlings farm, but seemed to accept her story about ordering some special flowers to surprise her cousin.

The road was dry as dust and deeply marked with wheel ruts which made her ride so bumpy in places, she swore she could feel her teeth rattle.

"Now I know why people ride horses around here," she said aloud, after one bone-crunching divot sent her nearly flying over the handlebars. She finally came to the homestead's driveway, which was marked by a rusty horseshoe nailed to a post on either side of the narrow passage.

Reece's house must be set far back from the road, because the driveway went on forever until finally she rounded a curve where the narrow drive opened up to a long, narrow strip of land, home to a small cottage and several outbuildings, one of which she assumed was the barn, judging by the wagon tracks leading toward it. On the cabin's opposite side stood a large hothouse, the roof crisscrossed with an interesting pattern of ridges. A stone's throw from the first hothouse, she saw the skeletal outline of what looked like a second structure.

She was so busy taking it in, the peaceful scene backdropped by a blue sky stretching as far as the eye could see before it dipped out of sight, that she didn't see the large, furry animal running frantically toward her until almost too late. As she swerved to miss it, her feet flew off the pedals and she lost control of her bicycle. It careened wildly toward the hothouse, the mangy mutt nipping at the vehicle's back tire and growling.

Oh no! As she neared the structure, the ground started to slope and she picked up speed at an alarming rate, the pedals spinning far too fast for her to get her feet back into position.

Straight ahead loomed the hothouse and she started to close her eyes, anticipating she and the bicycle would crash right through the glass structure. Suddenly a man stepped directly into her path, grabbed hold of the handlebars and brought the bicycle to an abrupt stop that sent her tumbling from the seat to land at his feet.

With a grimace of pain, he tossed the bicycle to one side as she scrambled to her feet.

"Be careful with that," she snapped, as she slowly moved her arms and legs to make sure she was still in one piece.

Reece Rawlings glared at her from an intimidating height. She hadn't realized the other day quite how large he was. Large enough to dwarf most men. Without a word he patted his leg and the dog ran to his side, sat at Reece's feet and eyed Chelsea with curiosity.

"You're dangerous," Reece said finally before he turned and started to walk away, the dog following.

"It was all your dog's fault," Chelsea said, stung, as she picked up the discarded bicycle, relieved it was none the worse for the encounter, and rushed to catch up to him. "He came out of nowhere with no warning bark or anything."

"He can't bark."

"What's with a dog that can't bark?"

Reece turned then and eyed her. "What's with all the questions?"

Chelsea caught her lower lip between her teeth. "I'm sorry. I came to thank you for the other day and—"

"I don't want to be thanked. I want to be left alone." As he spoke, Chelsea saw him favoring his right side, holding his arm bent at the elbow and close to his middle.

"Now I need to thank you a second time whether you

wish it or not. If not for you I surely would have crashed straight into that hothouse of yours."

"I was protecting what is mine." His dark eyes grew even darker at his words.

With little thought to his own safety. What kind of man did that?

A highly unusual one, came her brain's automatic response. An intriguing one, at that.

As Reece resumed his pace, the dog dropped back beside her and she instinctively reached down and scratched the top of his head.

"I wonder which of us was most alarmed?" she asked the canine. "You by me or me by you?" The dog blinked up at her. His muzzle was gray, which meant he was getting on in years.

"Neither of us likes strangers on our land," Reece said.

"How did he lose his bark?"

Once again Reece gave a pained sigh as he turned to face her. "He was mistreated by his previous owner."

Chelsea sucked in her breath. "That's awful!"

"Anything else?" As he drew himself to his full height, she noticed he winced. A faint scar marked his jawline, stark white against the dark stubble shadowing the lower half of his face.

Impulsively she laid the bicycle down and moved to his side. "You were hurt stopping me and my runaway bicycle." When she reached toward his injured arm he batted her hand away, but she saw the way his teeth clenched and his face whitened at the movement.

"Yes," Chelsea said as they faced each other in what was quickly looking like a stand-off. If it became a full-on stare-off he would win for sure, but for now she gave it her best.

"You asked if there was anything else, and the answer is 'yes'."

He didn't even blink. "I want to know about your setup here. What you grow besides flowers. Who are your customers. And where you gained your knowledge and experience. What are your plans for expansion?"

No expression crossed his face. He didn't move a muscle.

"Like Henrietta's people, my family owns vineyards in Argentina. These have been common dinner table topics since I was a youngster."

One corner of his mouth tightened. "You're not in Argentina anymore." He turned and resumed his stride.

Once more she scrambled to grab up her bicycle and jog beside him.

"That's exactly the point," she said. "The similarities. The differences. It all makes fascinating reading."

"Reading for who?"

"Oh, you know. People who are fascinated by other places. Other countries. Other cultures and traditions."

"People need to mind their own affairs." As he spoke, he clumped up the front steps of the cabin, went inside and slammed the door.

Chelsea cast a longing glance in the direction of the hothouse. She could see green leaves pressed against the glass and wondered what sort of exotic delights could be found inside. She imagined how it must smell, warm damp earth and exotically fragranced plants.

Since she wasn't snoopy by nature, merely inquisitive, she gave the dog one last pat on his head and mounted her bicycle. Before she pedaled off, she darted a quick look over her shoulder toward the cabin, convinced he stood inside watching her to make sure she left.

"You got your way this time," she said out loud, "but rest assured you've not seen the last of me."

HERE IN BULLET, Chelsea was soon feeling every bit as stifled as she had back home. She'd accepted a dinner invitation to the Copper Moon Ranch and met Henrietta's extended family members, but every time she thought she might have found something newsworthy to write about, like the heavily guarded home established by sisters Rose and Lily as a haven for wives escaping a bad home life, Henrietta kindly but firmly gave it the kibosh.

"Do you ever wonder why Ben is immediately on the heels of any strangers who come here? He's helping keep the women safe and the place's location secret, in case someone's husband tracks them this far."

Chelsea nodded. It was becoming very apparent she had led rather a sheltered life and had a lot to learn about the big, ugly world out there. Inevitably her thoughts circled back around to Reece Rawlings. He didn't strike her as dangerous, but he certainly was a man with a past and a secret or two.

More out of boredom than inspiration, she penned a short, humorous, partly true, partly fiction piece about touring areas of the Wild West on a bicycle, mentioning the bad roads and adding in the part about being spooked by a dog that can't bark, which she planned to mail to *Bicycling World*.

Truth was, although she'd grown used to the curious stares when she rode her bicycle around town, she found the horse and carriage Henrietta had left at her disposal a far more practical mode of travel.

Because she didn't fully trust the US Mail, she personally handed the packet containing her *Bicycling World* essay to the stage coach driver and watched as he tucked it securely into the mail pouch that would be transferred onto the train in Yuma. Fingers crossed! Turning away, she nearly bumped into a stranger, a man she'd sensed watching her earlier, and a shiver snaked up her spine.

"Sorry to bother you," he said. "But I'm looking for someone, and wondered if you could help."

Chelsea gulped. Was the man facing her one of those husbands she'd heard chanced to show up from time to time, seeking the whereabouts of a runaway wife?

"I'm sorry," she said quickly. "I'm just new here myself. I don't know anyone."

He raised a brow. "Oh, I saw you handing off a mail packet, so assumed you must be a local."

Chelsea shook her head. Where was the sheriff when you needed him? Let Ben take this man's measure and give him his marching orders. She deliberately turned and walked in the opposite direction. A short distance away, she stopped and pretended to stare into the mercantile shop's window where she caught the stranger's reflection in the glass, still watching her. She hoped he wasn't staying at the hotel, and headed there to tell Henrietta about the encounter.

The second she set foot in the hotel she forgot about the stranger, for Henrietta was speaking to Georgina in a hurried, agitated tone.

"I tell you. Something is wrong. Reece should have been by before today. He knows I like fresh blooms every week."

Georgina nodded sagely. "No one's seen him heading to the train station either, which is not like him. The man is regular as clockwork. Maybe we should send Ben out to the ranch to check on him."

"He'd be furious to think we pulled the sheriff from his duties here in town. Braydon's tied up at the ranch or I'd ask him. Maybe you or I should go and make sure he's all right."

Chelsea heard all this with a sinking feeling in her stomach. It had been over a week since she'd been out at Reece's farm, trying ever since to ignore the nagging worry that when he stopped her runaway bicycle, he'd been injured worse than she'd suspected at the time.

"I'll go," she said quickly.

Both women turned to stare at her. "Are you sure?" Henrietta said. "You don't know your way around very well yet."

"I came across his place when I was out for a ride shortly after I arrived. Even met his poor dog that can't bark."

Henrietta looked instantly relieved. "Don't let on we were mother-henning. Just act casual."

"Of course. Be back soon."

As she fetched her horse and carriage from the livery, she realized that she forgot to mention the man at the stagecoach depot, relieved there was no sign of him as she drove through town. Maybe he'd left already.

CHAPTER 3

Reece cursed silently as he attempted to button his shirt with his left hand. Whatever he'd broken last week, collarbone was his best guess, hurt like the dickens and made it nearly impossible to get even the simplest things done around here. The makeshift sling he'd fashioned from a drying towel helped a little by keeping the arm immobilized, but made him feel like a cripple. An awkward, bumbling cripple at that.

His attention shifted from the buttons to the door where Hobo whined and scratched to be let out.

"You hear something, buddy?" He opened the door and the dog bounded out toward a horse and carriage pulling up out front. His eyes narrowed when he saw who was driving. *Her* again!

She caught her heel in the hem of her skirt, narrowly missing a tumble as she stumbled to the ground. To his amusement she turned and stared at the carriage as if it was somehow responsible for her graceless exit. By the time she swiveled her gaze back to him he had his lips pressed into a tight, disapproving line.

"You're trespassing. Again."

"Henrietta was worried when you didn't stop by the hotel. She sent me to check and make sure you're okay."

He blew out a breath. The Masons were a well-meaning bunch, but he wished they'd take the hint that he wanted to be left alone. As far as anyone back home knew he was dead, and he intended for it to stay that way.

"So now that you've seen with your own two eyes that I'm standing here on my own, there's no need for you to hang around."

He glared at traitorous Hobo who nudged her skirt with his muzzle, looking for attention. Wretched hound! He should have left him with that miserable excuse for a human the dog used to live with. Except he hadn't been able to do that.

His bad habit of trying to rescue anyone or anything who needed help continued to get him into hot water. Including the woman who even now came toward him, undeterred by his lack of welcome.

Her gaze zeroed in on his makeshift sling.

"I knew you got hurt the other day," she exclaimed. "Why didn't you say something?"

"No point," he said gruffly. "It'll heal."

"Did you at least see the doctor?"

"Nothing he could tell me that I don't already know."

Small white teeth that reminded him of pearls worried her bottom lip. "It's all my fault."

"One thing we're in agreement over."

He saw her eyes widen in understanding. "That's why you haven't been to the hotel. And no one's seen you in town. You can't drive with only one hand."

Hell he couldn't! It was all the other things he couldn't do. He stared down at his partly unbuttoned shirt. Shame the sight of a man's partially unclothed chest didn't send her running back to town.

"I can drive," he said shortly. Unfortunately, as he'd learned the hard way, he needed two hands to cut and arrange the blooms and sort them into order pails for his customers, or to pick the berries and citrus fruits that folks around here had gotten a taste for.

"But little else," she said as realization dawned. She deliberately turned her gaze toward the greenhouse then back to him.

"If you'll show me what needs doing, I'll help you get caught up."

"I don't want your help."

"Well, that's a shame. Because I'm here now and Henrietta would never forgive me if I left you stranded with the use of only one arm. Especially seeing the accident was my fault."

"It wasn't an accident," he said. "I knew what I was doing."

"With little thought of the possible outcome, I'd wager."

"Seemed preferable to picking shards of glass out of your pretty face." He bit his lip, wished he could take back his impulsive words.

She tipped her head, a half-smile playing with her full, red lips. "You think I'm pretty?"

"You favor Henrietta some. Not enough to be classed as beautiful, like her." There, that ought to take her down a peg.

Except, when she smiled at him like that, Chelsea truly was beautiful. And something stirred unexpectedly inside, something he'd believed had died back in battle.

"All my life I've looked up to Henny, wanting to be more like her, brave and adventuresome, so I consider that a huge compliment. Not only that," her tone grew brisk, "I know she'd want me to stay and help."

Hobo nudged her again with his nose. "See. Even your dog thinks it's a good idea."

He gave her an ungracious look. "Somehow, I don't see you as the type to get your lily-white hands dirty."

"Are you serious? I grew up in the vineyard next door to Henny and her brothers. All us kids were out in the blocks from an early age, helping in whatever way we could."

Reece gave a skyward eyeroll. The Almighty certainly worked in mysterious ways. He'd been asking, just this morning, for some sort of guidance as to how he could get things back on track around here. Henrietta's cousin landing on his doorstep was not exactly what he'd had in mind.

"So let's get started." She turned toward the greenhouse, giving him little choice but to follow along. No way was he leaving her on her own in there.

She pushed open the door and scampered in, clapping her hands the same way she'd done that first day in town. She spun in a circle, sucking in a deep breath that caused her bosom to expand and push against the buttons fronting her dainty blouse, and he cursed himself for noticing.

"It's even more lovely than I imagined."

He settled for an acknowledging grunt, but truth be told, he found her enthusiasm gratifying. He'd not had anyone in here before. And certainly never figured on anyone embracing the place the way he did.

"Citrus," she exclaimed, approaching a lemon tree, touching the fruit's unripe, bumpy skin reverently before she pushed her nose right up against it. "I've not seen a lemon or an orange in months."

"This crop won't be ready for a while," he said.

"Grapes!" She spied the vines and turned to him with a naughty grin. "I bet I could teach you how to make wine."

"I'll leave that part to someone else."

"The flowers are glorious," she said, as she made her way past raised beds brimming with roses, daisies, chrysanthemums and dahlias, all in various stages of growth and propagation to ensure a continuous supply. "What are those?" She pointed to a cluster of tall trees at the far end, his latest experiment.

"Figs, I hope."

"Wonderful!" she exclaimed. "You could dry them on drying racks in the sun. That way they'd last a long time."

He'd had the same idea when he'd first planted.

"All right then," she said. "Put me to work."

He'd be perfectly within his rights to send her packing. But he couldn't deny how dry everything looked. The wretched rubber hoses were heavy and too difficult to wrangle one-handed. Instead, he'd relied on the watering can, a painfully slow process by the time he filled it, watered a few plants and returned to the tap.

"You see those metal columns?" The items in question ran perpendicular roof to ground, the length of the greenhouse, ten rows of them.

"The ones supporting the roofing channels," she said, surprising him with her knowledge.

"There's a tap at the base of each one, which provides the water source."

She stared upward, shading her eyes from the sun. "I wondered why the unusual channels and ridges on the roof. You collect the rainwater and funnel it into the columns, which are hollow. I must say, that's brilliant. Is it your design?"

He tried to hide his pleasure at her praise. "Not entirely. I made a few adaptations to what we had where I grew up."

"You really know what you're doing. No wonder you've made this such a success." She waved an arm. "And you're expanding the operation by building a second hothouse."

"Eventually," he said.

As he explained how to attach the hose and how much to water each crop, she was mercifully silent, diligently following his instructions. The air in the greenhouse grew damp and misty moist, and after their drink the plants seemed to perk up right before his eyes. Maybe tomorrow he'd manage to cut what he needed, deliver some into town and take the rest to the train station in Yuma.

"I think that's it," she said at last, sounding actually disappointed when the last section had been watered. She bent down to turn off the water, but must have turned the tap the wrong way for the hose shot out of her hand and careened wildly about the greenhouse, spraying water everywhere, including at him. When they both lunged for the hose, it somehow became tangled around them, locking them together until he managed to tame it and aim the spray of water away from them.

Through his damp garments he could feel her pressed against him, her clothing clinging like a second skin. She glanced up at him, wide-eyed, a myriad of emotions crossing her face as she realized he'd reacted as would any male who found himself in close proximity to a warm-blooded, attractive female.

He instantly tried to extricate himself, which only made matters worse.

"Sorry," she said breathlessly as she tried to reach the tap, but she couldn't quite manage it with the hose still twisted about the two of them, cinching her even closer. Unexpectedly she burst out laughing.

"This reminds me of a game from when I was a youngster, when the jump rope became so tangled I couldn't move."

"Indeed." Beads of water danced on her eyelashes, which this close up, struck him as inordinately long.

"I feel like a menace," she said. "Inconveniencing you nine ways to Sunday since my arrival."

"You do tend to cause havoc in your wake," he said, looking away from the dark shadow where her nipples puckered against the water-soaked front of her white blouse.

"You're not the first one who's told me that."

"I'm not surprised." He raised the hose higher with his one good hand. "See if you can step free of the hose, one loop at a time."

He stood ramrod still as she placed her hands on his hips to steady her actions, eventually managing to free herself from their entrapment. She quickly turned off the water, then took the end of the hose from him, and slowly unwound it until he too was clear, avoiding eye contact. He watched the way she rolled the hose with a tidy skill that told him she'd done this many times before.

"Do you need my help with anything else today?" she asked, eyes still downcast.

"I think you've 'helped' quite enough for one day." Lord help him if he let her loose with the pruning shears!

After leaving her horse and carriage at the livery, Chelsea returned to the hotel, relieved her clothing had dried on the sunny drive back. She had no idea what Henrietta might think if she returned dripping wet.

Henrietta! In all the excitement, she'd forgotten that Henrietta was anxiously awaiting a report on Reece's wellbeing.

Indeed, Henrietta spotted her the second she set foot inside. "Well?"

"Reece—Mr. Rawlings has had a slight mishap, but he seems to be bearing up fine."

"What sort of slight mishap?"

"He believes he broke his collar bone. He's fashioned a makeshift sling to keep the arm immobilized while it heals."

"Has he seen the doctor?"

"He didn't seem to feel the need."

"How is he managing?" Henrietta said.

"I stayed to help with the watering in the hothouse," Chelsea said. "I believe I will go back earlier tomorrow and try to make myself useful."

Henrietta gave a relieved sigh. "That's wonderful of you, Chelsea. I'm sure he really appreciated it."

Chelsea felt herself coloring slightly. She wasn't sure 'appreciate' would be Reece's word of choice.

"He's so independent," Henrietta said. "Normally he refuses anyone's help. We can't get him to join us at the ranch for supper, and lord know we've invited him enough times."

"Yes, well—" She started toward her room, then turned back. "By chance, are any of your brothers-in-law skilled at building?"

"Blake," she said quickly. "He can make almost anything. Why?"

"I noticed today that Reece has begun work on a second hothouse."

Henrietta's smile was slow and knowing. "That sneak! He's such a private person. He never said a word to me about increasing his capacity."

"I was just thinking. Reece having a broken collar bone and all, he won't get any work done on the structure for quite some time. Do you think Blake would be willing to go over there and carry on until Reece is healed?"

"That's a brilliant idea! Everyone in town has wanted to do something nice for Reece as a thank you for his heroics when he first arrived."

"Heroics?" Chelsea asked.

"Um hmm. He had just arrived and was over in the park. Two young boys had fallen in upriver and were being swept away by the current. Luckily Reece is a strong swimmer. Without a thought to his own safety, he dove in and rescued both boys." She smiled at the recollection. "He wasn't pleased the way the entire town made a fuss of his actions and threw a big party in his honor. He doesn't take to being the center of attention, and since then people here have respected his desire to be left on his own."

"Wasn't it you who got him into the act of hothouse cultivation?"

Henrietta shrugged. "He turned out to be a natural. He hasn't said as much, but I don't think he was enjoying growing hay for the ranchers."

Chelsea also gathered Reece wasn't one to sit around idle. No doubt having one arm in a sling was driving him mad.

Her memory pinged. "I almost forgot. This morning, a strange man approached me down at the stagecoach depot. Said he was looking for someone and wondered if I could help."

"Did he say who he was looking for?"

Chelsea shook her head. "I didn't give him the chance. I told him I was a newcomer and didn't know anyone, myself."

"It's probably nothing," Henrietta said. "Maybe a miner looking for work."

Chelsea didn't know what the average miner looked like, but the man hadn't struck her as a laborer.

"But I'll mention it to Ben, just in case."

Later that day as she was crossing the lobby, she overheard Ben talking to Georgina. She didn't catch everything Ben said, but her ears perked up when she heard 'private investigator', and 'British military'.

Georgina's response was indecipherable, so Chelsea bent over and edged closer to the pair, pretending to fiddle with the buttons on her boots.

"And you believe it was Reece he was looking for?" Georgina's low voice reached Chelsea's ears.

"The physical description was close," she heard Ben say. "But the investigator specifically asked after someone with the surname of Rollins."

Chelsea swallowed a gasp. Rollins and Rawlings were close.

"Is he wanted?" Georgina asked.

Chelsea squeezed her eyes shut, unable to imagine the man she'd been with earlier today could be wanted by the law.

Suddenly the pair fell silent. She turned her head and glanced over to see them both watching her. With a nonchalant smile she rose and dusted off her hands. "Pebble in the toe of my boots," she said casually. "Off for a short ride before dinner. See you both later."

She sauntered slowly toward the door, hoping they'd

resume their conversation, but neither of them said another word while she was in the room.

Outside, she collected her bicycle and looked up and down the street in frustration. Clearly, the man Ben had spoken to wasn't staying at the hotel. On impulse she mounted her bicycle and rode toward the boarding house, where luck was on her side. The gentleman she'd seen earlier was walking away from the boarding house toward the stagecoach depot, carrying a small satchel.

"Excuse me!" Chelsea skidded to an ungraceful stop a few feet in front of him. He raised one brow as she dismounted and stood facing him, one leg on either side of the bicycle's frame and her skirt bunched up. "This morning, when you told me you were looking for someone, I wasn't totally honest with you, and I'm sorry. I don't normally deceive people, but one is taught to be wary of strangers."

"It's no matter," he said. "The sheriff has assured me the man I'm looking for is not in the vicinity."

"Shame you came all this way for nothing," Chelsea said. "Is he dangerous, this man you seek? Just in case he should show up at some later time," she added quickly. "A lady on her own can't be too careful."

"It's not the law looking for him," the investigator said impatiently. "His family was originally told he was killed in a war overseas. Recently they received new information that he may be alive. Possibly suffering memory loss, which explains why he never returned home."

"They must be worried if they hired you to look for him."

"It's more than that. There's a matter of an inheritance."

"Really," Chelsea said. An inheritance at stake. Most men wouldn't change their name and become a recluse under those circumstances. But Reece wasn't most men. And Chelsea didn't believe for one second that he did anything by chance. "I certainly hope you find him," she said.

"Now if you'll excuse me, miss, I've got a stagecoach to catch."

Belatedly, Chelsea realized her bicycle was blocking the man's path. "Of course," she said, wheeling it off to one side, where she stood deep in thought.

Finally, her mind made up, she mounted the bike and rode toward the telegraph office. That nice professor, the one she'd met on the boat ride here who had introduced her to his editorial contacts, might be able to help.

CHAPTER 4

Chelsea was up early the next morning and reached Reece's farm before there was any sign of life, other than a noisy rooster off in the distance. Not even Hobo greeted her. She parked the horse and carriage beneath a lone, spindly tree and sped off to get the watering done. The earlier in the day the plants were watered, the better for their roots. Or so she had been taught.

Today, she'd brought her sketch book, charcoal, and sketching pencils, hoping to make a few sketches of his operation. She was particularly intrigued by the watering columns, such a simple yet brilliant idea. After she finished watering and rolled up the hoses, she found an old stool stuck away in the far corner of the greenhouse, buried under a pair of very large gardening gloves, a watering can, some wooden flats, several clay pots and a trowel, which she carefully moved out of her way. She dusted the dry dirt off with her hand and settled in to draw, losing herself in her art and the fragrant peacefulness of her surroundings.

A peacefulness that was short lived. "What in tarnation do you think you're doing?"

She looked up to see Reece glowering at her while Hobo wagged his tail enthusiastically. At least someone was happy to see her.

"Good morning," she said. "I came out early to get the watering done ahead of the noonday sun."

"No one asked you to." He clumped over to her, his shirt mostly buttoned, dark trousers tucked inside a tall pair of rubber boots. She guessed they were easy to get on and off when limited to the use of one arm. His stubble was longer than yesterday, emphasizing the scar on his jaw. She guessed shaving was also something he'd forfeited for the time being. Come to think of it she'd never seen him totally clean-shaven.

"No one was around," she said innocently.

He squinted at her sketch pad. "Why are you drawing my setup here?"

"No particular reason," she said innocently, gathering up the pages. She still hadn't given up on the idea of a series of essays about his horticultural accomplishments in the desert. The professor, on learning she had a modest talent for drawing, had told her she had a much better chance of gaining interest in her writings if they were also illustrated.

"I thought you might need a hand with something other than watering," she said innocently. "The hose quite behaved itself today without your scrutiny."

She could have sworn he was working to bite back a smile. But a sense of humor would make him human, now, wouldn't it? Was it possible he was human? His eyes were a deep, indigo blue, with a faint fan of fine lines in the corners. The creases around his mouth suggested he'd once found quite a lot to smile about. His hair was damp, as if freshly washed.

"I'm managing fine," he said quickly.

"Henrietta will be relieved to hear that. The hotel has been without fresh flowers for several days. I imagine your other customers have as well."

His eyes bore into hers, and her fingers itched to sketch him, to capture that proud countenance, firm jaw, and unwavering gaze.

Their stare-off was interrupted by the sound of horses coming down the driveway.

"Now what!"

Two horses appeared, pulling a wagon driven by a man who looked vaguely familiar, and it seemed Reece knew who he was. He left the hothouse muttering under his breath about folks suddenly feeling free to drop in whenever they wanted. She rose and followed, the dog butting her leg in a bid for attention. She gave him a quick pat on the head and started in the direction of Reece and the newcomer.

"Blake. What brings you out this way?" Reece asked once his guest was within earshot.

Blake! Of course. She'd forgotten her conversation with Henrietta about the second hothouse.

Blake jumped down from the wagon. "Heard you'd had a mishap. Came over to give you a hand on the greenhouse you're building."

Reece swung her way and leveled an accusatory look. She stared off in the distance, pretending she was unaware of anything amiss.

"That's real neighborly of you," Reece said. "But I expect to be right as rain in a few days."

"I know from experience that broken bones take their own sweet time to mend, and trying to rush the healing or strain the injury only ends up taking longer." Blake reached into the back of the wagon and pulled out a carpenter's belt with a hammer and other tools hanging from it. "Besides, the ladies would give me grief. I'm here at their say-so."

He looked past Reece and caught sight of Chelsea for the first time. "Hello again, Henny's cousin. Anyone else tell you that you look just like her?"

"Thank you." Chelsea gave Reece a cheeky smile. "I've heard most men find her very beautiful."

Reece narrowed his eyes but Blake flushed in a really charming way. He'd struck her as shy when they met at family dinner at the ranch.

"Listen, Blake, I don't want to put you out. You have your own projects," Reece said.

"I'm here now," Blake said. "Why don't you show me what's what?"

Chelsea smiled to herself as the two men started over to the building site. Hobo was sniffing at the ground where Reece had been standing, then whined, catching Chelsea's attention. Only then did she see a folded piece of paper where Reece had been standing. Something he must have dropped.

She bent down and picked the paper up, frowning at his chicken scratch writing. It looked like names of flowers. He must have been coming to the greenhouse to start collecting some blooms.

She glanced over her shoulder. She'd love to get started helping, but sensed he wouldn't appreciate her efforts, so she hung back with Hobo, out of the way of the two men as they walked around the site of the second hothouse. She could hear the rise and fall of their voices, but no actual words they exchanged. From where she stood it looked like Blake was nodding a lot while Reece waved his good hand through the air.

At last, Reece turned and made his way back to where

she waited. He looked resigned. Maybe he'd come to terms with the fact that there's no shame in accepting a helping hand.

He stopped a foot from her side. "You couldn't resist blabbing around town about my injury, could you?"

"Henrietta was concerned. Along with a lot of other people."

"I don't cotton to folks poking around my affairs."

She thought again about the private investigator. No doubt Reece would throw a major fit if he knew someone had been asking about him, at least asking about someone with a similar name who bore him a strong resemblance.

She lifted her chin defiantly. "From everything I've seen and heard about Bullet, it's a town where folks care about one another, more than most places. A place where a total stranger might wow the town with his bravery when he saves two young boys from drowning. And the townsfolk want nothing more than to do something nice in return."

Reece blew out a displeased breath and pushed past her. Once inside the hothouse, he reached into his back pocket with his good hand, a puzzled look on his face.

"Looking for this?" Chelsea waved the paper she'd rescued in front of his face.

"Are you a pick-pocket now as well as a menace and a blabber mouth?"

"Admit it," she said. "You're getting used to having me around. Or you'd better. Blake doesn't look like he's going anyplace anytime soon, either."

"At least Blake's not constantly running off at the mouth."

"I don't do that, either. Just give me a task and I'll go about it so quietly you'll never know I'm here."

His answering snort told her what he thought of that.

"Listen," she said to his retreating back. "You need to start harvesting the mature blooms so the plants keep producing. You can't do that with only one hand. Show me what needs to be cut."

His look spoke volumes.

"If you don't trust me with the clippers, I'll hold and gather up the stems you cut. You can send me back with the ones for the hotel. As for the rest, what do you do? Take them to the train?"

At his reluctant nod she continued. "I'll go with you. I can help with the loading and unloading."

And hopefully get to know a little more about him on the trip to Yuma and back.

GETTING Reece to talk about himself proved more difficult than Chelsea had anticipated. He answered her questions with either a grunt or a one-word response, his "yup" and "nope" designed to discourage further conversation. Yet, the more time she spent with him, the more intrigued she grew. What sort of man deliberately cuts himself off from society, yet rescues a mistreated dog and saves the lives of two youngsters he doesn't even know?

She didn't let on to Reece or anyone else how much she looked forward to seeing him every day, convinced she could eventually peel away his layers and discover who he really was. Reece Rawlings or Rollins or whatever his name turned out to be was simply too intriguing a puzzle to leave alone. Plus, she had a staunch supporter in Henrietta, who seemed pleased to hear Chelsea was spending her time at the farm helping Reece.

Ever since that first day, he was in the hothouse ahead of

her and she wasn't sure if he didn't trust her on her own, or if he looked forward to her arrival. At any rate, he'd become far less snarly, and even trusted her to take some cuttings and start rooting a new flat of plants that would go into the second hothouse when it was finished. Given that, she was a little alarmed when she showed up one morning and the only creature around to greet her was Hobo.

She unwrapped the treat she had started bringing him each day, usually a piece of ham or bacon purloined from the hotel kitchen, and spoke softly as he woofed it down.

"Where's the mister, Hobo?"

The animal licked his lips and gave her a hopeful look, but when it appeared there were no more treats to be had, he turned and started in the opposite direction. Around back of the cabin, which was sitting on more of a rise than she realized, the land dipped abruptly, rolling down toward the river.

Hobo raced ahead while she made her way gingerly, hoping nothing had happened to Reece. The ground was dry and uneven underfoot. Reece could have easily lost his balance and taken a tumble, especially with the use of only one arm. When Hobo disappeared through what was barely a path through some scrubby underbrush she hurried to keep up, aware of the sound of water. Moments later she burst through the underbrush and came out on a pebbly river bank. And straight ahead—

Oh, my word! Reece stood waist deep, his back toward her as he first splashed himself, then dunked, to come up shaking water from his hair and face. She could see the pull of muscles through his back and shoulders as he splashed more water, one-handed, onto his chest and arms. Not far from the edge of the water was a pile of clothing, including his sling. With an impish smile, she crept forward, picked up the sling and raced back into the underbrush while Hobo splashed through the water to join his master.

Chelsea was enjoying the chance to watch him when he was unaware, far too much to feel the slightest bit of guilt for what basically amounted to spying. Was it her fault she'd been concerned? Her smile widened at the thought of his reaction when he realized his sling was missing, then faded the instant he turned around and started toward her, wearing not a stitch of clothing.

She had naively assumed he'd be in some sort of bathing costume, not parading around the great outdoors in the all-together. What civilized creature did that?

She quickly looked away, and when she dared look back, he was semi-decent in his britches, although they remained unfastened. The sling felt heavy in her hands as she watched the way he fumbled awkwardly into his shirt. Even at this distance she felt his frustration as he tugged at the uncooperative buttons.

Finally she could stand it no longer and pushed her way through the spindly growth toward the river bank. Her boots crunched on the gravel, warning him of her presence.

A myriad of emotions crossed his face before he managed a guarded, yet neutral expression.

"I suppose it's asking too much for a man to bathe in privacy," he said, before he caught sight of the sling in her hand. His jaw clenched and his mouth tightened in a rigid line. "What game are you playing this time, Chelsea?"

It was the first time she'd heard her name on his lips. She liked the way it sounded, his British accent giving it a possessive ring, as if she was *his* Chelsea.

"I'm sorry," she said, suddenly ashamed of her actions. "Hobo led me here and at first I was afraid another accident had befallen you. When I saw you were fine, I thought it would be funny to tease you, let you wonder what happened to this." She stared down at the toe of her boots. "But it wasn't funny. It was wrong. And I'm very sorry."A lengthy silence stretched between them until she finally raised her eyes to meet his.

"You must have got yourself into a fair bit of trouble when you were younger. You're very good at apologizing."

"I'm far from perfect. And I have no problem admitting when I'm in the wrong. Like now."

"You must have been wrong a lot, given your penchant for blundering in where you're not invited and wreaking havoc."

"Being impulsive does seem to be one of my faults."

"Along with not listening?"

"I hear fine," she said, stung. "I just sometimes interpret things a little differently from others."

"So I've noticed."

She saw the way he cradled his right arm against his midsection as he tried to button his shirt. The sooner he had the sling back on, the better. Before she could rethink her impulsive action, she reached out and deftly fastened the buttons of his faded, plaid work shirt. Her fingers faltered on the top one, aware of the warmth of his skin through the fabric, the movement of his Adam's apple as he swallowed thickly, an unfathomable flash of emotion in his eyes. He reached up and clasped her wrist with his good hand, his fingers forming a tight circle.

"Leave it," he said, his words husky, his breath feathering over her face and stirring the tendrils of hair clinging to her forehead. "I never button the top one."

She stood frozen, one hand against his chest, the other imprisoned in his grip. His skin smelled clean from the river, and with his dark hair slicked back against his skull his other features appeared more prominent, emphasizing his potent masculinity. Something stirred inside her feminine reaches. He was so close, so undeniably male, she was overcome by an unexpected longing for something she hadn't known was missing from her life.

"I—I didn't know." Her breath caught. She scarcely dared breathe, as for one insane second she saw his head dip toward her and thought, hoped, he might kiss her. Instead, he released her and held out his hand for the sling.

"I feel crippled enough without being encased in this."

"It's important that you heal." She ignored his request and set to work fastening the sling into place, careful not to jostle him, amazed her hands were steady enough to secure it with a knot that was tight enough to hold it in place but loose enough that he could unfasten it easily with his other hand.

Sling in place, she followed him up the rise to where, under Blake's capable hands, the second hothouse was slowly taking shape.

Reece was relieved to see Blake as he reached the crest of land from the riverbank, aware of Chelsea dogging his heels. Spending every day in Chelsea's company was unsettling him. And not just because he preferred his solitude, but because she was starting to get under his skin, prompting feelings long buried to slowly come back to life.

When she'd reached to button his shirt, the caring gesture was almost his undoing. He couldn't recall the last time anyone had done something thoughtful for him. Most people respected the walls he'd resolutely erected around his life and his heart that didn't allow him to care or be cared for. The problem was he did care, too much. Precisely why he'd walked away from his family, his old identity, and reinvented himself in the new world.

For her part, Chelsea acted like there were no barriers, visible or invisible, a situation that was dangerous for both of them. Especially today when he was overcome by the urge to kiss her. The other sad truth was that she was an entertaining helpmate. He was continually astounded by her wealth of knowledge and questioning mind. As they worked, she seemed to know intuitively when to ask questions and when to stay quiet, and in truth, he'd never before met a woman who knew how to keep quiet for more than a minute.

Hobo adored her and had taken to standing by the door each morning, watching for her arrival, his eyes lighting up when he heard her coming down the drive. Reece shared that same quiet spark of pleasure anticipating her company, even though he didn't run to her in excitement the way Hobo did.

"Morning." Blake greeted them both as if there was nothing unusual seeing them coming up from the river. "There's just a couple of things to finish up, then I can't do anything else until you get the glass."

"Glass won't be here for at least a month," Reece said. "You got to this point way faster than I would have."

"Well, let me know when the glass gets here and I'll give you a hand installing it," Blake said.

Reece swallowed the uncomfortable feeling in his gut that rose up his throat at the thought of being beholden. "Thanks, but I'll be able to manage."

"Just because you can, doesn't mean you ought to," Blake said. "Storm's on to me about you coming for supper on Sunday after mass."

Mass! It would be a frosty day before he set foot in a church anytime soon.

"Both of you," Blake added, looking at Chelsea. "Reece, you haven't experienced full Bullet hospitality until you've come to one of our family gatherings."

"Blake's right," Chelsea said. "We wouldn't miss it."

Reece blew out a breath. "You have no right to speak on my behalf." His words sounded harsher than he intended, leaving him feeling cornered, aware of Chelsea and Blake exchanging a look. How to refuse without looking churlish? "Very well then," he said with poor grace.

"Storm's inviting Percy and Hope as well. She thought you might feel a little more comfortable if there was another familiar face."

It would take far more than a familiar face for him to feel comfortable in their group. He'd had no idea when he got here that the Masons were such a tight clan and a force to be reckoned with, en masse or on their own. Otherwise, he probably would have settled some other place. Lord knew there were lots of choices in the West.

The Masons would never understand the real reason he kept his distance, for the family reminded him of everything he'd left behind. Deliberately, but still causing an achy twitch from time to time. Being alone out here was easier than being alone in the midst of a crowd where he didn't belong.

"Good," Blake said. "Glad that's settled."

CHAPTER 5

Chelsea absently thanked Storm, Blake's wife, as the other woman slid a cup of tea in front of her after dinner at the Mason's ranch. How could the rest of them sit through dinner so calmly? Weren't they fuming inside the same way she was?

For Reece had taken the cowardly way out, snuck over here while the family was at mass, and left a big bunch of flowers and a note saying he wouldn't be able to make it tonight after all. His cowardly act was nothing to do with her, but she was embarrassed none-the-less. How dare he?

The flowers were displayed on the sideboard, their delicate perfume a potent reminder that some people had no manners. If it had been up to her, she would have happily taken the blooms outside and stomped on them, the way she'd like to stomp on Reece's head.

"Feels like we're in for a cold one tonight," said one of the Mason twins seated across the table. Chelsea hadn't yet figured out Henrietta's extended family members and who belonged to whom, including several rambunctious toddlers running around. When she tried to puzzle which of the identical twins was married to which of the two sisters named after flowers, her head started to hurt.

She hoped Reece was cold, lonely and miserable with only Hobo for company. Served him right! But as the conversation about the weather and its effect on the local farmers swirled around the table, she had another thought. How would Reece keep the hothouse warm enough throughout the night? She'd seen the coal furnace just outside of it, and knew which piping ducts brought in warm air when the cool desert nights threatened the safety of Reece's exotic plants. But there'd been no cold snap since she got here. He'd not had to deal with stoking the furnace using only one arm.

Across from her, Percy and Hope stood. "Are you ready to go?"

"Of course." She stood as well and thanked everyone for making her feel at home. She would have preferred to drive out to the ranch on her own, but Henrietta had displayed an unexpected mother-hen side, insisting it wasn't safe for a woman alone on the road at night.

She liked Henrietta's friend Percy, a successful hunter of lost treasures and his wife, Hope. As the carriage ate up the miles into town, she mentally kicked herself when she suddenly recalled Henrietta mentioning some sort of connection between Reece and Percy years ago. Blake had made a similar remark the day the invitation had been issued.

She leaned forward and wedged her face between the two front seats so she could speak with the others. "What's with your friend, Reece?" she asked Percy. "It seems rather poor form to leave a last-minute note saying you won't be coming after all."

"I don't know the bloke well," Percy said. "We met up by

accident, two Brits stumbling across each other in the middle of nowhere, and joined forces for a while. I don't think treasure hunting appealed to him the way it did to me, or to Henny when she joined me years later. Reece and I parted ways amicably enough, but I must say I was surprised when he showed up in Bullet."

"No reason for him to be here?" Chelsea asked.

"Just said he was tired of moving around and that a small town like this, miles from the closest railway line, suited his needs. I knew old Bowles and his wife were tired of the farming life, so I introduced Reece to them and next thing I knew he had bought their farm."

Chelsea sat back. Interesting, but it left her no closer to figuring the reclusive man out.

Back in her room, she pulled out her sketchbook and flipped through the pages where she had created several crisp, concise examples of Reece's set-up, complete with the hollow support columns to collect and distribute water. It had little to do with the *Western Travel* essays she had originally intended to write, but was a topic she found eminently more interesting, and something she thought would appeal to a wide reading audience.

When he wasn't looking, she'd managed to capture Reece's likeness in several different poses, and she flipped through them with a critical eye. Not half-bad if she did say so herself. She'd done a good job of capturing his proud arrogance, underscored with an occasional hint of vulnerability, all of which made him a most fascinating subject. As she rose to turn up the lantern and draw the blinds, she glanced into the garden which lay mostly in darkness except a wide swath lit by a single beam of moonlight. Frost glittered on the leaves of the plants illuminated by the moonlight. She placed her hand flat against the window pane, and pulled it back immediately. If her window was this cold, she could only imagine the frigid temperature inside the glass hothouse.

Without further thought, she changed into her riding bloomers and bundled into her warmest cloak before she retrieved her bicycle from the maid's storage closet in the hall. Outside the hotel, a kerosene lamp hung on either side of the front door. Chelsea hoped Henrietta wouldn't mind her borrowing one to hang on the front handlebar of her bicycle to help guide her way. Anyway, with luck, she'd have it back before morning. She'd driven to Reece's so often these past weeks she ought to be able to find her way blindfolded, but no point leaving things to chance.

As she mounted and set off, she turned a deaf ear to the memories of her father's mocking voice echoing in the darkness, saying she'd never amount to anything. She could still hear her brothers' shouts of laughter stating she wasn't even suitable marriage material. Shortly after that, she'd made secret arrangements to travel to the new world, vowing to never return.

She was relieved to not pass a soul on her way to the farm. All she needed was to run into one of Henrietta's many relatives and have the story filter back to her cousin.

Finally, she reached the turnoff and jounced down the rutted driveway to where the farmhouse lay in darkness, fingers of frost painting the peaks of the roof. She quietly rested her bike against the spindly tree where she normally parked the carriage, grabbed the lantern off the handlebars and headed for the hothouse.

In this case, the hothouse had become the cold house,

her breath fogging in the cold night air. Someone had placed strips of burlap over the flats of seedlings and shoots, as well as wrapped burlap over the beds containing the delicate citrus and fig trees, no doubt Reece's attempts to protect the plants from the cold night air. Burlap had also been applied to the lower trunks of the rose bushes, but there were no protective measures in place for the daisies, chrysanthemums, dahlias, zinnias and a host of other flowering plants.

She took the lantern outside to the Franklin Stove, which was already set to light. Except for the lack of safety matches. Reece probably had them inside with him. Luckily, there were a few tightly rolled spills tucked in with the kindling and she carefully ignited one from the flame beneath the chimney of her lantern, then transferred it to the kindling, relieved when the small pile of starter caught quickly, allowing her to add a generous scoop of coal from the scuttle. By the time she was done, her fingers were numb from the cold and as she rose, she blew on them to warm them with her breath.

As she picked up her lantern to go inside and make sure the heat was being channeled through the heating ducts, she froze. Reece stood a few feet away, a rifle tucked between his waist and the elbow of his good arm.

REECE COULD NOT BELIEVE his eyes!

He'd been woken by a swatch of moonlight shining through a chink in the curtains, and when he got up to adjust them saw a light bobbing around in the dark, near the greenhouse.

At the foot of the bed, Hobo stirred as he pulled on trousers and a thick jacket, but happily wagged his tail and laid his head back down at the sound of Reece's voice. Reece, meanwhile, slipped his feet into his rubber boots, grabbed his rifle and crept out the door toward the light.

"What in thunderation are you up to now, woman?" He lowered his rifle as he spoke. He could shoot left-handed if he had to, but was glad it hadn't come down to that. He'd much prefer to throttle this particular uninvited visitor. "Are you aware it's the time of night when decent folks are in their beds?"

"I was worried about the plants in this cold snap."

"So I see." He stood there eyeing her in the faint light afforded by her lantern as she worried her bottom lip.

"I'm sorry I woke you. I only intended to light the stove and get it stoked up to warm the air in the hothouse."

"What if you left and the fire went out? Are you aware you'd do the plants more harm than good with sudden temperature fluctuations?"

"I wasn't going to just up and leave."

His cynicism kicked in. "What? You were planning to stick around all night and keep the fire going?"

"Probably. At least until the sun rose."

He could tell by the way she stared at the ground that she hadn't thought things through. Did she ever?

"Do you have any idea what your cousin would say when you got back to the hotel if she found out you'd been out here with me all night?"

She shook her head, eyes wide on his, as if gauging his mood.

"Well, I don't feel fancy being yanked out of bed with a shotgun pointed at my head, forced to marry someone I don't even like, all because her reputation has been tarnished."

"Henrietta wouldn't do that."

"You can't predict just what the Mason brothers might do, given the circumstances. What would happen back where you come from?"

He could tell his words hit home when Chelsea blew out a breath. "I never thought—"

"You need to learn to think."

She flinched as if he had struck her, raised her chin in that stubborn way he was coming to know. "I've been told I think too much. And that no man will ever have me because of it. That no man will ever want me, period."

As he digested not only her words but the emotional way she recounted them, he wondered what other lies she'd been fed. And what else might have happened back home that sent her halfway around the world. She had no more common sense than an infant, coupled with a stalwart belief in her actions, right or wrong. That kind of compulsive behavior could land a woman in a heap of trouble. He also knew he couldn't send her home alone in the dark.

"Well, you've started this now." He went over and kicked the near-empty coal scuttle. "The coal box is in the shed with the wood. You may as well make yourself useful and fill it up before you go."

To his surprise she did his bidding without an argumentative word while he headed inside the greenhouse. He hated to admit it, but she'd been right. A dip in temperature this low overnight would wreak havoc with most of the plantings, especially the new seedlings just being propagated.

Fool woman was lucky she'd not been accosted on her

way through town to get here. Nothing for it but him seeing her safely back to the hotel. And hope like hell the Masons never heard of her nocturnal visit.

He looked up to see her standing in the doorway watching him, the moment fraught with tension. She reminded him a little of Hobo when he'd rescued him from that brute. Unsure if he was going to a better place or someplace worse.

"You were right," he said begrudgingly. "I was remiss not to put the heat on earlier in anticipation of the temperature drop."

Her face lit up like the sun coming out after a storm. "I couldn't sleep for worry." Abruptly her smile faded, her expression closed off. "That was most cowardly of you earlier, that note you left at the Copper Moon about not coming for supper. The least you could have done was deliver it in person. And if you'd been there, you would have heard about the cold front headed this way. I could have gone home and fallen asleep knowing you had things taken care of."

Reece couldn't believe this chit of a young woman dared to give him, a veteran soldier, a man of the world, a man of British nobility, a piece of her mind. "So you being here in the middle of the night is somehow my fault?"

"In a word, yes."

She crossed her arms over her chest as she spoke, her eyes sparkling with temper.

Words escaped him.

"They all like you," she said, her voice softer now. "They just don't understand why you're so standoffish."

No, they wouldn't. Letting people close meant exchanging confidences, perhaps unwittingly revealing his past. No one here would understand how he could go on letting his family believe he was dead.

"You saved those boys from drowning. You're a hero in the eyes of everyone here."

He'd never wanted to be a hero. He only ever wanted to help. The crux of things was; it was impossible to help folks, and at the same time expect to be left alone. Helping folks was a big part of who he was, at odds with living like a hermit. Which is why he'd agreed to grow Henrietta the flowers she wanted for the hotel, never dreaming it would become a fulltime occupation. Or lead to a situation like this. Henrietta's cousin looking at him with those big, serious eyes. He shivered and turned away before he did something stupid.

"I should get you back to town. I'll just stoke up the fire first."

"I can make my own way."

He turned on her then. "Just because you can, doesn't mean you should. A woman alone can't be too careful. Henrietta was attacked once on this very road. Did she ever tell you that? Kidnapped by some ruffians."

Chelsea's eyes grew wide. "I never knew that."

"Well don't be asking her. Or telling her you heard it from me. Percy let the story slip once, then immediately regretted it. I pretended not to hear."

"But—"

"No buts." He looked past her to the tree where she normally parked. "Where's your carriage?"

"I rode my bicycle."

Reece felt as if a cold hand reached inside his chest and clenched his heart in an iron grip. "You did what?"

"I was hardly going to the livery in the middle of the night to collect the carriage." She said it so matter-of-factly,

Reece had no response. He went outside and stoked the stove, Chelsea trailing in his wake.

He stood. "I'm going to get the wagon. Stay here and try not to cause any more problems."

She opened and closed her mouth a few times, as if she had a lot more she'd like to say, then finally nodded.

CHAPTER 6

The town was still in slumber when Reece deposited her at the hotel. After he'd lifted her bicycle from the rear of the wagon he climbed back in his seat and stayed there, holding the reins in his good hand while he watched her replace the borrowed lantern. Once she'd unlocked the front door, she jockeyed her way inside, holding the door open with her foot as she pulled her bicycle in after her. Locking the door behind her, she stood with her nose pressed to the window as he slowly turned the wagon around and headed out of town.

A frosty silence had hung over their trip into town. Hard to tell if he was mad at her, but she didn't care. She was mad at him, and she didn't even know why. It was more than him declining a meal with the Masons. It was— She couldn't figure him out. Even when he admitted she was right, something didn't ring true.

He'd been right on one count. If the menfolk in her family had got wind of her being alone with a man in the middle of the night, the two of them would either be dragged to the altar or the man would be swinging from the end of a rope. She'd thought things would be different here. That women would have more choices. More opportunities. Yet it seemed the final say still always rested with the men.

"There you are," Henrietta said later that day, as Chelsea returned from a light lunch at the café. "I feel like I've hardly seen you since you arrived."

Chelsea gave her cousin a half-smile. "Didn't supper yesterday count?"

Henrietta pulled a face. "The Masons are quite the crowd when we all get together. Hardly conducive to a private chat. It reminds me a little bit of home, but in a good way. There's something to be said for a family where we all support each other instead of tearing each other apart." She must have noticed Chelsea's pensive look, for she pulled her over to a private corner in the lobby with a settee and a side chair and chose the settee, leaving Chelsea the chair. "How are you settling in, really?"

Chelsea shrugged. "Fine, I suppose." It was a bald-faced lie. She'd completely lost her focus for traveling here in the first place. What happened to asserting her independence? Working on her essays with the goal to seeing them published? Really, truly experiencing life here in the West.

"I take it you've been spending a fair bit of time helping Reece."

Henny didn't know the half of it. She'd be scandalized to learn Chelsea had gone out to his farm in the middle of the night. Or would she? Surely it was no different to some of her cousin's treasure hunting exploits. And what about what Reece had said about Henny being kidnapped? Chelsea was dying to hear more about that adventure.

"Aren't you mad at him?" Chelsea asked. "For not showing up yesterday?"

"I'm sure he had his reasons. Which brings me to a delicate topic. Reece was here earlier with my delivery."

That Chelsea helped him cut and gather. *Oh, no! He didn't—he wouldn't have mentioned last night, would he?*

"He's made a request through me that you not go out to the farm any more. He's removed the sling and says he's managing just fine." Henrietta's gaze remained locked on hers. "Please don't embarrass me or yourself by ignoring his wishes."

Chelsea blew out a breath. "I don't feel like I belong anywhere. Not in my old life. And not here either."

"You need to give it some time," Henny said kindly. "Get involved locally. See if Storm can use a hand at the library. Volunteer to sing in the church choir."

Chelsea pulled a face. She hadn't come halfway around the world to help in a library or sing in church. She could have done both those things at home. "How did you manage to escape?"

Henrietta's brow wrinkled. "Escape?"

"The world over, it seems most women wind up in a life where they have children to raise and husbands who tell them what to do. But not you."

Henrietta's expression grew sad. "One day, you may feel different. That marriage and children is not as bleak as it sounds."

"But you—"

Henrietta took her hand. "I very much long to have a child. And I try not to look too enviously at those around me who have been blessed with a family. So far, Braydon and I have not been successful in that endeavor."

"Oh."

Henrietta released her hand and rose. "Fortunately, the

hotel keeps me busy and I get to play aunty to my nieces and nephews."

Chelsea sat back in her chair, deep in thought. She'd assumed Henrietta's life stood for everything a modern woman could want. A handsome husband who didn't berate and belittle her, a thriving business, freedom to do and go as she wished, not saddled with offspring. And yet—

"Miss Diaz?"

She started, not having had anyone here address her by her surname. "Yes?"

The youngster held out a paper. "Telegram, miss."

As he took a step back and rocked on his heels, Chelsea realized he was waiting for some coinage. She fumbled in her reticule and passed him the first coin she touched.

His eyes lit up with surprised delight. "Thank you, miss," he said before he ran off.

She stared at the telegram for a minute, relieved it hadn't arrived from back home as she hadn't told anyone where she was going, but from her professor friend in the East.

Dear Miss Diaz,
As you know, I do adore a puzzle, so set out forthwith to see what I could learn about your friend, Rollins, or Rawlings as you claim he now calls himself. There is indeed a Duke of Rollins. The second son, Luke, inherited the title when the older brother, Reece, who was reportedly killed in the line of duty in Perak, died without issue. How interesting to learn that a stranger would be making inquiries. The plot thickens, as they say. I will check with my military cohorts and see if perhaps they can shed a little light on things. How goes the wordsmithing?
Yours,
Winthrop

Chelsea read the telegram a second time before she folded it and placed it in her reticule. The plot had indeed thickened. She rose, unwilling to wait around to hear from Winthrop. She didn't care what Reece had said to Henny. She was determined to hear the truth from the man himself.

Outside the hotel, she stared in consternation at the spot where she was certain she'd left her bicycle leaning against the wall. She looked on the other side of the door in case she'd been woolgathering when she returned from lunch, but the conveyance was no place in sight.

She looked up and down the street, not certain what she was expecting to see. Everyone in Bullet knew the bicycle belonged to her. Perhaps someone had taken it for a joy ride and would show up here at any minute, shamefaced and apologetic. Except no such occurrence happened.

As she stood there wondering what to do next, a wagon pulled up and a buxom young woman Chelsea recognized from the hotel dining room jumped out.

"Miss!" She rushed to her side. "I just saw a strange man on your bicycle. Riding toward Yuma."

"What the—" Someone *stole* her bicycle! The nerve! And heading for Yuma, no less.

"Thank you so much!" Without a second thought, she raced to the livery, collected her horse and carriage and headed for Yuma, pushing Henny's poor horse to his limit. The thief might have a head start, but she was determined to catch up.

Unfortunately, she reached Yuma without overtaking whomever had made off with her bicycle. It seemed pointless to drive up and down the streets looking for him, but what other choice did she have?

Glancing about in frustration, she suddenly spotted her bike being pushed by a scruffy, unkempt stranger going into the train station. In the distance she heard the train's whistle, announcing its approach. She secured her horse and raced through the depot, looking about frantically until she spotted the thief at the far end of the station.

The platform was crowded with people waiting for the train to pull in and she was jostled from side to side as she hurried after him. She was still some distance away when the train arrived, the doors opened to discharge a horde of travelers, and she lost sight of the thief with her bicycle.

REECE ARRIVED in Yuma just as the train's whistle blew in the distance. He was right on time. It would take more than a few minutes for the new arrivals to clear the platform and the depot, and even longer for those departing to find their way on board. He pulled his hand cart from the back of the wagon, wincing as the movement jostled his still-healing injury. He'd likely jumped the gun removing the sling too early, but he didn't know how much longer he could take seeing Chelsea every day and listening to her inquisitive chatter.

She was a pest and a nuisance, he reminded himself. Hobo had sulked all morning, ears pricked as he listened for her arrival, morose when she didn't appear. Reece kept busy, refusing to admit that he felt much the same, missing her ready smile, her tinkling laughter, the diligence with which she applied herself to whatever needed doing.

The porters were too busy to help, so he made his way to the refrigerator rail car, opened the door and started loading in his buckets of blooms. When they were all in, he climbed in after them and situated them safely against the far wall, away from the other perishable items being shipped in the cold compartment.

He'd never known a woman could be a helpmate as well as an agreeable companion. His betrothal to Ann had been something planned by their parents pretty much since the two of them were born. A way to combine the two families' estates and ensure the next generations became even wealthier and more powerful. He'd found Ann pleasant enough company in a bland, unexciting way. Like most young ladies of her station, she'd been schooled to lay an attractive table, play the piano in a somewhat palatable fashion, and run a household smoothly.

They'd never been alone together. She'd never buttoned his shirt or shown the slightest interest in how he filled his day. He'd never watched the way the sun kissed the tip of her nose through the greenhouse glass, or the shadow her thick, dark lashes cast upon her cheeks. Or noticed the different shades of pink and vermillion staining her full lips, lips that he longed to capture beneath his own, anticipating her quivering response, the mingling of their breath as—

What in all things good and holy was she up to now?

He jumped down out of the refrigerator car, slammed the door behind him and strode along the platform to where Chelsea appeared to be attacking a lone male holding her bicycle hostage. Before he reached the pair, the man quickly turned the tables, one arm locked around her middle, his other hand grasping her bicycle as he dragged her kicking and flailing toward the train as the warning whistle sounded.

Reece broke into a run as the man attempted to board the train, dragging both Chelsea and her bicycle. He reached the pair just as the man struggled onto the step, attempting to push a flailing Chelsea ahead of him. Reece grabbed the stranger by the shoulders and yanked him hard. The man swore, spun in shock, dropped the bicycle, but tightened his hold on Chelsea.

He didn't think Chelsea even saw him. She was too busy fighting off her attacker with a well-placed elbow to the ribs and a mighty stomp to the man's instep before she leaned forward and bit his hand.

The man yowled and flung her to the ground just as Reece got in the act, bending the man's arm behind his back until the fellow shrieked in pain. The scrawny bloke proved no match against Reece and eventually ceased his struggle, sending glaring looks to where Chelsea was picking herself up from the ground.

"Go and get the sheriff," Reece called.

She straightened and seemed to see him for the first time. Her brow wrinkled, her mouth opened as her gaze moved from him to his prisoner and back to him. "Go!" he said. The man had stopped fighting for now, but Reece's still-mending collar bone was aching something fierce.

Luckily Chelsea was back in mere minutes, a man with a star on his chest close on her heels. The man he held made one last bid for freedom, but Reece tightened his grip. As the pair approached, Reece caught the occasional word Chelsea threw at the sheriff. "Thief. Chase. Kidnapped."

"Well, well. What have we here?" the sheriff said. "If it isn't Slim Jim, wanted for bank robbery in several states." The sheriff commandeered the prisoner and slipped a pair of shiny metal cuffs around his wrists. The man glowered, first at Chelsea, then at Reece. "I guess we'll add bicycle theft to the list, will we, Jim?"

"Stupid town. Doesn't even have a bank," the robber said.

"So you stole my bicycle instead?" Chelsea said.

"Needed some way to get back here. Besides, I thought it would come in handy for a quick getaway, go places horses couldn't follow."

"Tell it to the judge."

Reece bit back a laugh. Was the fellow serious? Where did he think the bicycle would take a rider that a horse couldn't follow?

As the sheriff thanked them for their help in apprehending a wanted man, adding someone would be in touch about the reward, Reece turned to Chelsea. "Seems I can't let you out of my sight for a minute, that you don't stir up all sorts of trouble."

"Thank you for coming to my aid."

"Are you joking? I was starting to feel sorry for the bloke. Where'd you learn to fight like that?"

"My brothers were forever picking on me. I had to learn a few tactics for self-preservation."

As the sheriff left with his prisoner Chelsea rested her hand against his cheek, and it was all he could do not to turn his head slightly and press a kiss to her palm. "How's your injury? This must have made it worse."

"Nothing I can't handle." He reached down and righted her bicycle with his good hand, sucking in his breath, and vowing he'd be back in the sling the second he got home.

He looked at the poor bicycle, its rear wheel buckled. "You won't be riding this anyplace right now. I suggest you get Blake to take a look at it when we get back. I'll bring it in the back of the wagon. How'd you get here, anyway?"

"I brought the carriage."

So they wouldn't be traveling back together. For some reason, the thought didn't make him as happy as it ought to. Out in the street, he placed the bicycle carefully into the wagon bed. Who knew, on that fateful day he first laid eyes on this woman and her contraption, the kind of impact she'd have on his life?

Her eyes on his were big, dark pools a man could drown in. "Do you think he really would have kidnapped me and held me prisoner?"

Reece couldn't speak due to the knife blade twisting in his gut at the thought of what might have happened to her if he hadn't been there.

"Maybe we could hitch my carriage and horse to the back of the wagon and I'll ride with you. That way, I could spell you if your collarbone starts to give you grief."

She didn't want to be alone.

And for the first time since the war, neither did he.

CHAPTER 7

They must have made an amusing sight leaving Yuma, with her carriage secured to the back of the wagon, and her horse tied to one side. It was slow going covering the miles to Bullet, and Chelsea wasn't sure if that was for safety's sake or because Reece felt as reluctant as she did to part ways later.

"We're much alike, you and I," she said. "Both having left our families behind to start a new life here." She was dying of curiosity about the inheritance Reece had also left behind, and why someone had been hired to find him.

"My father and brothers always told me I'd never find someone foolish enough to agree to wed me. Papa didn't anticipate the way I turned the tables on him after he said that." She peeked sideways to make sure Reece was listening. "I told Papa, since I was so unmarriageable, there was no point him hanging onto my dowry, he might as well give it to me to make a fresh start. I knew Henrietta liked it here, so I thought why not give it a try myself? I had no other place in mind to carve out a new life. Of course, it's nothing like I thought it would be. I'm not even sure what I was expecting..." Her voice trailed off.

"Sorry," she said. "Talking helps to calm me when I'm agitated, and take my mind off of what just happened. Or almost happened. I mean, what I imagine might have happened. And really, I can only just imagine because I've never—"

"Sounds like you've been pretty much agitated since the day you arrived."

She bit back a smile. "Are you saying I talk a lot?"

He just grunted, eyes on the road ahead, darting from side to side as he drove. Was he expecting more trouble?

"Fancy that bank robber showing up in Bullet, only to find out we don't have a bank in town. I wonder why Ben didn't spot him and run him out of town right away? How do you think he got there in the first place? I mean, did he walk there, and that's why he helped himself to my bicycle?"

"He probably caught a ride with someone passing through, only to find out there's no bank he could rob."

"I suppose." She placed a gentle hand on his knee nearest her, the one that was almost but not quite brushing her leg. She inched closer along the bench seat toward him, wondering what it would feel like if he put an arm around her shoulders? Of course, such a move would be impossible because of his injury—

"Is your broken bone feeling worse? Do you want me to drive?"

"Would you stop talking if you had the reins?"

"Likely not."

"Then there's no point, is there?"

But she heard the smile in his words and gave in to temptation, leaning against him and leaving her hand where it was. He felt reassuringly big and solid, and a sense of peace stole through her. "Thank you for coming to my aid back there." She turned her head to look up at him and touched the scar on his jaw. "How did you get this?"

His lips thinned. "Happened in the war."

"Did you always want to be a soldier?"

"I hate injustice. Sometimes fighting back is the only way to ensure change for the better."

Chelsea nodded. "Have you ever lost your memory? Even for a short time?"

He stiffened. "Why do you ask?"

She shrugged, trying not to look guilty of prying. "Just thinking how awful such a loss must be. They say, at the end of our days, our memories are all we have."

"I remember things just fine. Even things I'd rather forget."

Chelsea snuck a sideways look. Did he mean the war? Or did he mean his family back home? As much as she'd been happy to leave, she still had many fond memories of her younger years.

"I have a confession to make," she said.

"Oh?"

"I wrote an essay about your hothouse design and sent it to a periodical back East."

Again, she felt him tense against her. "You had no right to do that."

Words tumbled over each other in her haste to reassure him. "You needn't worry, I didn't mention your name or even what part of the country it was in. But I felt it could be of benefit to others and I know you like to help so—" She twisted her hands in her lap. "I didn't have to tell you," she added defensively. "But I don't want half-truths between us." She looked up at him, opening her eyes their widest. Maybe her being so forthright would spark something within him. If it hadn't been loss of memory that saw him walk away from his title and inheritance, what was it? For in her heart of hearts, she believed he was the man the professor had told her about. The man other folks were looking for. The man who didn't want to be found.

In a totally unexpected move, he leaned toward her and brushed the top of her head affectionately with his chin. She heard his exhaled breath, felt it warm on her scalp as his chest rose and fell, almost as if he was tired of fighting. She curled closer and looped her arm around his middle, secretly relieved when he didn't move away, or ask her to.

After a few blissful minutes she tilted her head toward him. "Am I hurting you?"

His eyes were dark and unfathomable, glinting with an emotion she'd never seen in his gaze as he shook his head.

They arrived at the Copper Moon ranch and slowly drew apart. Did he feel as reluctant as she did to move away? She climbed down, already missing the warmth of his body next to hers as he unloaded her bicycle.

"Blake's shop is over here."

Besides the original ranch house and the seven cabins, each occupied by one of the brothers and his family, the ranch land had half a dozen outbuildings and barns. She trailed along, sad to see the full extent of damage to her bicycle. "Do you think Blake will be able to repair it?"

"Haven't seen anything yet he wasn't able to fix."

"Reece." Blake came out of the shop, wiping his hands on a greasy rag. "What brings you here?" His eyes widened at the sight of Chelsea. "The two of you." It was almost two questions; like why were they here and why were they together?

"Little mishap with Chelsea's bicycle."

Blake took hold of the item and ran his hands over the frame and the wheels.

"Do you think it can be repaired?" Chelsea asked anxiously.

"Never worked on one before, but don't see how it's much different than straightening a wheel on a carriage or a wagon," Blake said.

"Appreciate it," Reece said.

"Where should I take it when it's fixed?" Blake asked. "The hotel or the farm?"

Chelsea glanced at Reece and saw he was waiting for her to speak. "Whichever you find most convenient."

Blake nodded and headed back into the shed, carrying the bicycle easily in one hand.

Reece turned to her. "Can you make it back to town all right from here?"

"I could," Chelsea said. "But I'm not. I'm coming back to the farm to help you. Don't tell me your injury isn't worse. I can tell from watching the way you move."

His eyes narrowed. "Seems to me, folks have been known to see what they want to see."

She planted her legs apart, arms crossed over her chest. "What do you see when you look at me."

"Trouble," Reece said slowly and distinctly. "I see nothing but trouble."

CHELSEA COMFORTED herself with the thought that at least he didn't send her packing. Instead, he helped her back up in the wagon, turned it around and headed toward the farm. Once there, Reece took the horses into the barn. She peeked inside and smiled to herself when she saw he was feeding hers as well as his, as if it was something he did every day.

Meanwhile, she scampered over to the hothouse and got busy with the watering before pausing to check on the progress of her delicate new seedlings. She knew he was behind her even before he spoke. For the blood pulsed up and down her spine, while the skin on the back of her neck sparked from his nearness. She felt, or imagined she felt, the warmth of his breath on the nape of her neck, stirring the tendrils of hair that had escaped from her French roll.

She turned to find him every bit as close as she had imagined. She caught her breath, eyes wide on his.

Might he kiss her?

Was there something she should do to let him know she would welcome such an overture?

The air hung heavily between them, fraught with tension. Her limbs felt syrupy and weighted. He had really thick eyelashes, the tips curled in a way she could only envy.

"There you both are!"

They leapt apart at the sound of Henrietta's voice, then turned as she strode between the rows of plantings and reached their side.

Chelsea could not believe the calm tone of Reece's voice. "Henrietta. Were you looking for me?"

"Actually, I came to fetch Chelsea back to town."

"Why?" Chelsea asked.

"Simply put, Reece has made it abundantly clear that he does not want you here. The fact that you ignore his wishes and continue to impose your company on him both saddens and embarrasses me. That a relative of mine would behave in so brazen a fashion, insinuating her way where she is clearly not wanted." Henrietta punctuated her words with a huff that signaled either vexation or frustration. "Now come along this minute."

Reece's face broke into a huge smile, the likes of which Chelsea had not seen before. It gave her a clear picture of the man he must have been. Before the war. Before whatever happened to drive him into reclusion.

"Seems there's been somewhat of a misunderstanding," Reece said.

"But you said—"

"I spoke out of turn," Reece said. He gave Chelsea an encouraging smile that sent tingles racing from the tips of her toes to the top of her head, making her scalp all prickly. "At first, I worried about your cousin's reputation. I don't care a fig what folks think about me, but I was worried what whispers might arise if word got around that she was out here alone with me. But with Blake here more often than not, it's not like her reputation has been compromised. Truth is, I'm grateful for her help."

Henrietta's face relaxed into a puzzled frown as she glanced from Reece to Chelsea and back to Reece.

"Well," she said finally. "I'm glad to hear Chelsea is making herself useful."

"Did she tell you about her writing project? The one she sent back East?"

Henrietta continued to look perplexed. "She mentioned wanting to write about people's experiences in these parts."

"You needn't talk about me as if I'm not here," Chelsea said. "I had hoped to write about life in the West, and I still might, but it will be my own experiences, not those of others. In the meantime, I became fascinated by Reece's system for water delivery in the hothouse and thought it would be helpful to others."

"Water delivery." Henrietta glanced around, clearly at a loss at the sudden turn in the conversation.

"Reece is far too modest by half," Chelsea added. "Earlier today he saved me from a bank robber who stole my bicycle and tried to kidnap me."

Henrietta's jaw dropped.

Chelsea rested a possessive hand on Reece's good arm. "I'm afraid he worsened his injury by removing the sling too early and tangling with the would-be thief."

"Mercy! Where did all this happen?"

"In Yuma. At the train station."

Henrietta blew out a breath. "You have completely lost me."

"It's rather a long story," Reece said, taking Henrietta's arm. "Why don't you come up to the house? I'll fix you a cup of tea and explain everything."

"I'll just finish up the watering and be right there," Chelsea said. "Henrietta, make sure Reece puts his arm back into the sling."

"I'll be sure and do that."

Chelsea bit back a smile at the look on Reece's face. As if the world as he knew it was careening out of control. A look she recognized because she felt the exact same way.

After tea, Henrietta refused to leave until she extracted a promise from Reece that he would be there for family dinner on Sunday.

"I want Ben and the others to hear the full story from you," she said as she mounted her horse.

"Am I invited?" Chelsea asked cheekily.

Henrietta pulled a face. "Family is always welcome."

Chelsea turned to Reece as Henrietta galloped down the driveway. "That's nice. She included you, also, as part of the family."

Reece raised a brow. "Masons have a habit of adopting strays."

"You're hardly a stray," Chelsea said. "Private investigators don't scour the country making inquiries about strays."

"What did you just say?"

"I—Uh. Nothing."

His eyes narrowed. "Don't lie to me, Chelsea. You distinctly said something about a private investigator."

She pressed her lips together, cast her eyes downward for a moment, then looked up to meet his gaze. "There was a stranger in town awhile back. Claimed to be looking for someone. He spoke to Ben. Apparently, the name and physical description were a close match to you, but not exact, so Ben sent him on his way."

Reece blew out a breath.

"Were you the one the investigator was looking for?" Chelsea asked. "I'll quote you here. Don't lie to me, Reece."

"Lots of men in these parts match my description."

Personally, Chelsea disagreed. She'd yet to see another man come close to matching Reece in size, coloring, or distinctive bearing. With a name too close to be a coincidence.

She felt sad that Reece didn't trust her enough to tell her the whole story about who he was and what or who he was hiding from. That pervading sense of sadness stayed with her the entire way back to town later. Worse yet, it eradicated the warm, close feelings she'd felt building between the two of them earlier in the day.

CHAPTER 8

Reece parked the wagon and strode into the sheriff's office. Chelsea's disclosure yesterday had plagued his thoughts ever since and made sleep last night impossible. How on earth had someone tracked him here? He'd thought he was safe in his new life. Maybe even safe enough to start entertaining plans for the future. Plans that may or may not include a certain dark-haired woman who talked far too much for her own good. But right now, he was grateful for her slip of the tongue.

To the best of his knowledge, everyone believed he had died in the line of duty. So what had changed? And who was on his heels? Close enough that they'd come this far.

He pushed through Ben's open office door and closed it behind him with a click. "Hoped I'd find you here." This was not a conversation he wanted to have out in the street, which was where he usually ran into Ben.

Ben stood and reached to shake his hand. "This is a surprise. What can I do for you?"

"Understand you had words with a private investigator

awhile back. Fellow asking questions about someone who might look a little like me."

Ben sat back down, leaned back in his chair and crossed one knee over the opposite leg, one booted ankle resting on the opposite leg.

"Where'd you hear that?"

Reece leaned forward, weight supported on his good arm, palm flat on the desk, not in the mood to play games. "It's a small town, Ben. Word has a way of getting around."

Ben pressed his lips together. "Apparently it does."

"So?"

Ben shrugged. "Name he mentioned was close, but didn't match. Same with the description. I don't know what he wanted or who sent him. I do know we look after our own here. I didn't see any point in steering him out to the farm, maybe have him dig around, unearthing something you'd rather stay buried."

"Even if I was a killer?"

"That would be different," Ben said. "According to the investigator, the man he was looking for hadn't done anything wrong except disappear without a trace. Kin back home wanted to make sure he was all right." Ben met his gaze. "I don't have kin other than my people here but if I was to disappear, I expect they'd turn over ever rock on the planet trying to find me. Only because they care. If you've got someone who cares that much, count yourself lucky."

Reece straightened. "Thanks, Ben. Appreciate the straight goods."

Ben nodded. "Anytime."

~

CHELSEA SAT on the end of the Mason family pew. As the choir began to sing "Here I am Lord", she picked up her hymnal and stood, along with the others, just as Reece appeared at her side. She immediately shuffled sideways to make room for him and tilted the hymnal so he could see the words. Henny glanced over at her, nodded and slid closer to her husband, Braydon, making more room.

It appeared Reece was joining them for more than the main meal afterwards, and his unexpected presence sent a warm rush of pleasure through her. She barely heard the sermon, distracted by his broad shoulder nudging hers in the close confines. As they stood or kneeled at the appropriate times, she snuck the occasional sideways glance his way, but his eyes remained straight ahead, focused on the crucifix high on the front wall.

She was pleased to see he was wearing a tailored jacket and had made the effort to shave. He looked years younger without the dark stubble shadowing on his jaw. One more tiny glimpse of the man he used to be.

At last the service was over, the recessional hymn, "With Joy Let Us Go" particularly fitting. She was joyful to be outside, milling next to Reece on the outskirts of the Mason clan. Not only did Henrietta's relatives appear to know everyone in town, the other churchgoers seemed keen to extend their well wishes, while Chelsea was happy to shrink into the background alongside Reece.

"Thank you for joining us," she said. "I feel much less of an interloper now that there are two of us."

A faint smile played with his lips. Lips that appeared fuller and redder than she recalled. Seeing her gaze on his lips, Reece tugged uncomfortably at his tie. "I forgot what it was like. Being part of a well-known, well-respected group of townsfolk."

Chelsea took that to mean that his former life had been of a similar societal make-up, and wondered again what had driven him away and why.

As the crowd around them thinned, she was aware of Ben and Georgina off to one side, heads bent close together, intent on a private conversation. Normally she wasn't one to eavesdrop, but today the usually unrufflable sheriff spoke in irritated tones and punctuated his words with agitated hand gestures. Whatever he was saying clearly upset Georgina. The other woman's eyes were suspiciously shiny as she shook her head vehemently.

When Ben's voice rose, Reece and Chelsea made eye contact. They had both heard Reece's name. Deliberately Reece took her arm and guided her closer to the couple.

"You are the only one I told," Ben said. "I expected better than for you to say something to any of the others."

"I didn't," Georgina said. "I swear to you, I didn't."

Ben stood with his hands on his hips, his lips thinned with disapproval as he faced his wife.

Reece kept hold of Chelsea's arm as he approached the other couple. "Don't mean to interrupt folks," he said.

Ben swung around. "I'm having a private conversation with my wife."

"I respect that. I just wanted to make one thing clear. My visit to your office the other day was not sparked by anything I heard from Georgina."

Ben straightened. "You said it yourself, word has a way of getting around. Has to start somewhere."

Chelsea spoke up quickly. "In this case, the blame lies with me. I overheard you at the hotel one morning, telling Georgina about the investigator. The same man had approached me earlier, so I sought him out to ask who he was looking for, and why."

Reece's expression darkened as he turned to Chelsea. "You spoke with the man yourself? Yet deliberately gave me the impression that he'd only talked to Ben?"

Chelsea nodded. "I was—I was hoping you'd trust me enough to tell me the truth."

"Me? Share things that are none of your concern? When all you've done since you got here is interfere and cause trouble?"

"I didn't mean to," Chelsea said, eyes downcast as she bit her lower lip.

Reece turned to Ben and Georgina. "I'm sorry your misunderstanding was indirectly my doing."

"I'm sorry, too," Chelsea said.

She turned away, keenly aware of a strained silence between Ben and Georgina, and hoping their lives were not irreparably damaged by her carelessness. That was clearly that. Reece's short-lived foray back into society, or sorts. He'd no doubt order her to never set foot on the farm again. And she'd never know who he was. What a cock-up she'd made of things, trying to start afresh in the new world.

"Is that your bicycle?" Reece asked.

Odd question, since it was the only one in town. "Yes. Good as new thanks to Blake."

To her surprise, Reece plucked up the bicycle and headed to where his wagon and horse waited. Once there, he placed the bicycle in the back and turned toward her. "Are you coming?"

"Coming where?"

"The ranch. Family supper. Don't tell me you've forgotten already?"

"I—no, I—" Chelsea hurried to catch up. "I wasn't expecting you to offer to drive me."

He picked up the reins as she climbed into the front seat

next to him. "No doubt you expected I'd be so cross with you that I'd light out of here, back to the farm and refuse to ever speak with you again."

"Something like that," Chelsea mumbled.

"Which is no more than you deserve," Reece said. "Except for one thing."

"What's that?"

"I've been discontent for a while now. Unable to put my finger on the source of that discontent. After all, this is the life I chose for myself."

"I don't think it is," Chelsea said. "I think it's the life you wound up with, largely due to circumstances beyond your control."

He sliced her with his gaze. "Think you know things about me, do you?"

"Perhaps."

"The danger with you, my dear, is whatever you don't know, you're more than likely to concoct in that very fertile imagination of yours. Before that happens, allow me to set the record straight."

Chelsea narrowed her gaze. Was he offering to tell her who he was? And what sent him into reclusion?

HE'D EXPECTED to pique Chelsea's curiosity, and his impulsive decision surprised even himself. With a sense of resignation, he acknowledged it was time. Time he was true to himself. And hiding away, cutting himself off from others was not his nature. He had been raised a warrior, a fighter, a helper, the best kind of soldier. The kind who sacrifices himself for the good of others. Which is also what he had done on his brief return to England.

"I was involved in a battle. One of many overseas, but this time was different. This time I was wounded, and woke up with no idea of who I was or where I hailed from. The others in my squad were all dead. There was no one there who knew me."

"Didn't you have, I don't know, some sort of identification?"

"Everything was lost. And so was I. Nothing was familiar. After the hospital patched me up, a kind couple took me in. They were getting on in years with no family of their own, so I helped on their farm. And eventually bits and pieces of my past started to come back, but in a teasing way. Were my memories real? Or simply wishful thinking? Fragments of dreams? Before too long the old couple passed away and I decided to follow the clues and see if I could find my way back home.

"Which I eventually did. It was all as I recalled. The estate. The countryside. Even my old dog, who had been nothing but a pup when I left. Except he answered to a new master, as did everyone in the household and the surrounding area. My younger brother Luke, believing I was dead, had inherited the title, the estate, and the woman I had promised to marry. I saw them together once in the distance. It was obvious she was in a family way. And I knew at that moment that my return would be more than awkward. No good would come of hurting the people I loved the most.

"I loved my brother. I heard good things about him from those who knew him, how he was a devoted husband, a more than fair employer, and I decided then and there to leave and never return."

"Somewhere along the way you met Percy."

Reece nodded. "Another Brit on a self-imposed exile.

Except he was clever enough to make a new life here and I was dead set on keeping to myself, despite the best efforts of the most tenacious Mason clan."

"You didn't have to tell me all this, you know. But you have my word it will go no further." Her eyes widened. "Who do you think is behind the private investigator?"

"I admit, that part worries me some. But I'm no longer willing to stay hidden, to live in the shadows. I was spared in that battle for reasons known only to The Almighty. By keeping to myself, I'm doing Him a disservice."

He felt Chelsea's small hand grip his knee in an urgent way. "You're not at all."

"What have I done to make the world a better place?"

"You saved two young boys from drowning. Boys who will grow up to be men and fathers. You stopped a thief in the act and turned him in to the authorities, thus sparing other victims. You supply exotic fruit and vegetables to the people nearby, to say nothing of your flowers that bring beauty to the lives of others."

"You make me sound far more noble than I am."

"I speak nothing but the truth. And I for one am looking forward to meeting this man you told me about. The soldier who has made untold sacrifices."

Her small, slim hand was still on his knee, as if it belonged there. He covered it with his own. "So am I."

CHAPTER 9

This time at the Mason family gathering and meal, Chelsea didn't feel like an outcast. With Reece at her side, she got to know a little more of the other family members. The room was full of not only laughter, but of love, something that had been sadly missing from her life in Argentina, and she was relieved to see all seemed once more roses and sunshine between Benjamin and Georgina.

When Percy said something about Henny that made the entire roomful break out into laughter, she smiled shyly up at Reece, who chose that exact moment to meet her gaze. As their eyes met, it felt like they were the only two people in the room. Her heart sped up so fast she could scarcely breathe.

"Are you all right?" Amanda, whom she recognized as the pianist who had accompanied the choir earlier, was on her other side next to Amanda's husband, Bradley. A quiet man, all she knew about him was that he was reputed to be gifted with animals. She'd met men like that back home, men more comfortable in a stable or a barn than around people.

"Fine, thank you. Just a little warm all of a sudden. What's your son's name?"

"Sam," Amanda said proudly. "He's only three and already trying to read."

Storm, the town librarian, leaned across the table. "They're never too young to learn to appreciate books."

"Agreed," Chelsea said.

"Henrietta said you intend to write some essays for publication."

"That's right," Chelsea said, proud she had something to contribute to the conversation. All these folk were so busy and so accomplished, it would have been intimidating not to be able to hold her own. "I was told that including illustrations makes my writing more interesting to the periodicals."

"Short stories?" Storm asked.

"Perhaps at some point I'll try my hand in that area. Recently, I mailed a piece to *Bicycling World* about owning the only bicycle in a small town, and one to *Lipcott's Magazine* about Reece's clever method for gathering water in his hothouse. I didn't mention which part of the country the greenhouse was in, only that it was in the desert. I think it will capture the interest of gardeners everywhere."

"I guess Ross wouldn't let you write a piece about the workings of the mine, would you Ross?" Storm said.

"I doubt the safety measures I've recently installed would garner much interest. Unfortunately, most mine owners are hungry for profit, first, last and foremost over worker safety."

"That's true," said Ross's wife, Janie. "But you could write an entire book about Blake's many talents. You should see the wonderful cooker he built for my bakery."

"I'm already a fan after he fixed my bicycle which was damaged when it was stolen."

Not everyone here had heard the story about the robbery and attempted kidnapping, and as Chelsea recounted the day's events, embellishing it for dramatic effect, she was pleased when Reece jumped in and added his personal anecdotes to the story. She was particularly delighted to hear him express disdain for the thief and terror at what might have happened had he not been at the station at the same time.

"You'd better watch it, Reece," Brody, the town mayor and head of the family said. "You're going to get a reputation around town as the man everyone can count on to come to the rescue."

"I've got no problem with that," Reece said. "I've never been one to back down from a challenge."

"Not even from me," Chelsea teased.

He gave a half-amused look that took her breath away. "Tenacious little thing. You cause havoc at every turn and refuse to take 'no' for an answer."

"Sounds like someone else I know," Braydon said with a pointed look at Henrietta. "These hard-headed women from foreign countries."

"Everyone here came from a foreign country at one time or another," said one of the twins.

"Not really," said the woman on his far side, whom Chelsea assumed was his wife. "The natives were living here long before the whites arrived."

He dropped a kiss on the top of her head. "I stand corrected, darling wife. We are the newcomers."

More banter ensued, and the afternoon passed all too quickly. A wonderfully fun camaraderie made all the better by Reece taking part.

As they offered up their thanks and goodbyes afterward, along with the various guests and family members, Chelsea sighed. She'd never experienced such a satisfying day and was reluctant to see it end. She faced Reece at the side of his wagon.

"Who knew you had quite the sense of humor under that gruff exterior of yours?"

He gave a jerky nod. "It's been a long time since I've found much to smile about."

"I'm glad to see you haven't forgotten how."

"So am I."

Suddenly, Chelsea realized they were alone. The other guests had driven off, and the Mason's had each returned to their respective cottage. She eyed her bicycle in the bed of the wagon. She wasn't looking forward to a long, lonely ride back to town, or an even lonelier evening in her hotel room.

"Do you—do you need a hand in the hothouse before it gets dark?"

"I can manage, thank you."

"I guess that means you don't need my help anymore."

"Actually, I don't. Which is not the same as to say I don't want your help."

All Chelsea heard was 'don't want your help'.

"Fine, then," she said. "If you don't mind taking my bicycle out—"

"Do you feel like riding back to town?"

"Not really," she said in a small voice, as she focused on the buttons on the front of his shirt. They had a pearly sheen to them, outlined in silver.

His thumb butted her chin, forcing her to look up at him.

"What do you feel like?"

She moistened her lips. "I'm not sure."

"Well, I am. I feel like kissing you. But only if you find the idea agreeable."

"Agreeable!" she squealed, launching herself at him so he staggered backward a few steps to regain his balance with her in his arms.

His mouth curved in a slightly crooked smile she found so endearing, now that she was getting used to seeing it. He gave his head a gentle shake as if he couldn't quite believe what was happening. Then he lowered his head and captured her lips with his own.

His mouth felt divine, his lips firm and warm and possessive as they explored hers. She sighed in pleasure at the flood of warmth that suffused her limbs, and he immediately coaxed her tongue to tangle with his. She could feel his body's strength at every juncture, her softness cradling his leanly muscled chest and legs. She wiggled slightly in an effort to draw even closer, tightening her arms around his neck.

She could feel the slight abrasion of his afternoon whiskers against her chin, and longed to feel that same tingly delight on other parts of her skin. But that would mean his mouth abandoning hers, a thought she couldn't bear as she deepened the kiss, holding him as close as possible and chafing at the layers of clothing between them.

Reece was the one who eventually ended the embrace and put her an arm's length from himself. Chelsea's eyes flew to his. Had she done something wrong?

"Not a thing," he said heavily.

"How did you know what I was thinking?"

"Your thoughts are clearly visible on your face. One only needs to know how to read them."

Her eyes twinkled as she took a step closer. "I'm not sure I like that. Am I not allowed any secrets?"

He blew out a breath. "Are you keeping anything from me?"

She slowly shook her head, her eyes on his. “You from me?”

He shook his head as well.

“Then that’s settled. We shall always be forthcoming with each other, and never have a misunderstanding.”

“You underestimate human nature. Folks tend to jump to conclusions on a regular basis. Look at Georgina and Ben. At loggerheads through no fault of their own.”

“We shall be more careful.” As she spoke, she reached his side and slid her arm around his middle. Slowly and deliberately, he removed it.

“We must do things the proper way. As they are your closest relatives, I shall state my intentions to Henrietta and Braydon and seek their approval to spend time with you.”

“Please tell me you’re not angling for us to have a chaperone,” she said drily, secretly thrilled by his words, for she wanted that also.

“I think we’ve moved beyond the chaperone stage,” he said. “But I wish to make it clear I am not trifling with your attentions.”

She raised her head in a silent challenge. “And if I rather like being trifled with?”

“You are incorrigible,” he said, taking her hand. “Come we will speak to them right away, while we are here.”

Once Henrietta and Braydon got over their surprise at Reece’s request, Braydon shook Reece’s hand. “I hope you know what you’re in for. These South American women are a force to be reckoned with.”

Henrietta gave his arm a loving tap. “You know you wouldn’t have it any other way, my love.”

Braydon smiled down at his wife, his face awash with love for her. “I’m afraid that’s true. A meek and mild woman would bore me senseless.”

As the men switched topics to Reece's expanded hothouse business, Henrietta took Chelsea aside. "Are you sure this is what you want? Reece is the first man you met when you arrived in town."

"Quite certain," Chelsea said. "He intrigued me from the start, and the more I got to know him—"

"He's always been very closed-mouthed about his past," Henrietta said.

"I know everything I need to," Chelsea said. "But it's for him to share, not me."

"Just because he is courting you, doesn't mean you are stuck with him forever," Henrietta said. "Take things slow and get to know each other, first."

"The way you did with Braydon?" Chelsea asked cheekily.

"Our circumstances were—unusual," Henrietta said.

Chelsea glanced fondly to Reece. "I could say the same."

"As long as you're happy," Henrietta said. "From what I've seen, he's a good man."

"Ironic, really. I didn't come West looking for a man, but to discover who I am. Somehow, spending time around Reece taught me that and so much more. The future is full of unexpected possibilities."

Henrietta gave her a quick hug. "Which is exactly the way it's supposed to work."

EVEN THOUGH REECE was fully healed and no longer in need of her help, there was no talk of her not showing up at the farm each morning full of energy and ideas and excitement, eager to see Reece, to spend more time in his company. No longer was she rebuffed by a scowl when he caught sight of her. Often he was already in the hothouse, but his face would light up, he would stop whatever he was doing and greet her with a kiss.

To her disappointment, their kisses remained chaste for the most part, despite her efforts to recapture the frenzy of that momentous first one, the way her knees went weak and blood spilled desire throughout her limbs. Yet the way his eyes darkened as they rested on her, or his hand lingered on her hip, she knew he was keeping a tight rein on his desires. And every once in a while she was treated to a hint of the passion that simmered just beneath the surface.

One particularly hot and sunny day as they toiled side by side in the hothouse she grew uncomfortably warm and unfastened the top buttons of her blouse, rolling the sleeves back to her elbows as she fanned herself with a piece of sketch paper. For she had taken to sketching everything she saw, luxurious blooms, Hobo snoozing in whatever patch of shade he could find, Reece, the occasional bird that found its way into the hothouse, even the river sluggishly making its way past the farm.

Reece shot her a look. "You should go inside where it's cooler. Blake is working to create some sort of cooling fan system to help keep the temperature more palatable on these hot summer days.

"I won't leave you out here," she said. "But I will tempt you to take a cooling dip in the river with me."

Reece shot her a look and they were both remembering that day she had surprised him bathing.

"I've swum in a pond on our property back home, but never cooled off in the river."

"It's too cold for you," Reece said. "And dangerous in places."

She sashayed toward him with her most seductive look,

one she had practiced in secret with the help of the looking glass in her room at the hotel. Lids half-closed, a come-hither tilt to her lips, not quite a smile, but an expression full of challenge and invitation. "What's wrong with a little danger?"

He blew out a breath. "Chelsea, you tempt a man to the end of his endurance. I swear you do it on purpose."

She fiddled with the buttons on his shirt, slid two fingers through the gap. "Do what on purpose?" she asked with mock innocence, her head tilted back as she moistened her lips.

"This." With careful deliberation he removed her hand from his person. "You're a minx and you know it."

"They say Latin blood runs hotter than British," she teased.

He cocked a brow. "Are you saying I'm cold-blooded?"

"Not for a second. But it's fun to chip away at that British reserve you pull out around me."

"I swear on all that's holy, it is my one attempt at self-control around you. And a weak one at that." He pulled her into his arms. "I don't know if I should kiss you or spank you. Or both."

"But you intend to marry me."

"After a respectable amount of time passes for us to get to know each other better."

She ran her fingers through his hair, thrilling to its thick texture against her fingertips. "I can think of at least one way to speed up the process."

His eyes on hers darkened with lust. "Be careful what you wish for." Then he swept her up in his arms and carried her into the cabin, slamming the door on a hopeful Hobo.

CHAPTER 10

"Chelsea, will you please stand still?" Storm spoke around a mouthful of pins as she crouched at Chelsea's feet, pinning the hem of her wedding dress while Henrietta stood nearby, smiling.

"I'm sorry. I just— I can't wait to see how it looks."

"It looks beautiful," Henrietta said quietly, crossing to her side and smoothing back a strand of hair. "Just like you."

"I cannot believe Reece and I are soon to be married," Chelsea said, making a huge effort to not shift her weight from one foot to the other.

"I don't think Reece can either," Henrietta said. "He walks around like a man in a complete daze."

"Was Braydon like that the month before your nuptials?"

"I think I was the one in the daze," Henrietta said. "I honestly don't recall."

Storm straightened. "There you go. Slip out of it, please. Be careful not to stick yourself."

Chelsea poked out her bottom lip. "But I didn't get even a glimpse in the looking glass."

"I told you," Storm said, gathering up the layers of white froth as Chelsea wiggled free. "Not until it's finished."

Henrietta gave her arm a friendly squeeze. "Some things are worth waiting for."

"Like true love," Chelsea said.

"Exactly."

"Did I tell you Reece is selecting the blooms I'll carry on our wedding day? My bouquet shall be a total surprise."

"Only about a dozen times," Henrietta said fondly, as they left the downtown storefront where Percy's wife, Hope, designed unique articles of clothing that Blake's wife, Storm, when she wasn't at the library, and her helpers brought to life. Chelsea appreciated that Hope had listened closely to her vision of what her wedding gown should look like. She even took Chelsea's rough sketches, and from them created a pattern for Storm and the others to work with.

"I appreciate you lending me your veil," Chelsea said.

"Something borrowed," Henrietta said.

"I'm going to pop by the post master's and see if the mail is here yet," Chelsea said.

"You've been haunting the postal office lately," Henrietta said teasingly. "Are you expecting something special?"

"Maybe," Chelsea said. It had been months since she sent off her article and sketches about Reece's hothouse irrigation system. She'd received a brief telegram saying the periodical had found it suitable for publication and would forward her a copy once it was printed. Seeing her work out there to be read by others was not quite as exciting as her upcoming wedding, but a close second.

And because her life had been feeling so charmed of late, the periodical was there, wrapped in brown paper and addressed to her, along with a letter from Madre, which she opened first when they got back to the hotel. She quickly scanned the single sheet, the wording so stiff she suspected it had been dictated by Padre. She looked up to see Henrietta watching her thoughtfully.

"You told them about Reece?"

Chelsea nodded. "She wishes me well and declines to make the voyage here to see my new home."

Henrietta gave her shoulder a comforting squeeze. "Our mothers are very old-world, Chelsea. Bound to the dictates of their husbands."

Chelsea gave her head a shake. "Thank goodness we both broke out of that mold."

"Are you going to open that?" Henrietta indicated the brown paper packet with *Lipcott's Magazine* inside.

"Indeed I am." She picked up the letter opener from the hotel's front desk and slit the paper carefully so she could tuck the periodical back inside afterwards to keep it from wrinkling.

Her hand shook as she flipped through the pages. And there it was. right in the center, the sketch of the setup Reece had created, with her words in glorious black and white, boxed in on either side.

"Oh no!"

"What?" Henrietta peered over her shoulder and gasped. For there in the bottom corner, in an oval outline as if it was a photo frame, was a likeness of Reece.

"What has you two lovely ladies so aghast?"

Reece! Chelsea whirled, automatically clasping the periodical behind her back. "N—nothing."

Reece's gaze roved from Chelsea to Henrietta and back to her. "I told you before, your face hides nothing from me, Chelsea."

She sent Henrietta a pleading look for help, but Henrietta's eyes were still wide with disbelief.

Her heart clamored and her insides churned. If only the floor would open and swallow her, but no such mercy was delivered.

Reece's eyes narrowed as he waited.

"It seems a mistake has been made with my essay," she said.

"Surely it can't be that bad. Let me see."

Reluctantly, feeling herself on the way to the executioner's block, she passed over the periodical.

"Your first by-line." Reece smiled fondly until his eyes tracked to the lower corner and saw his own likeness.

He looked up at her. "Is this some kind of a joke?"

"It's a terrible mistake," she said, her hands knotted in front of her. "I have no idea how it happened." Behind her, she became aware of Henrietta melting into the background and leaving them in private.

"It seems fairly simple to me. You sent them in a sketch of my likeness which they decided to publish for the entire world to see. Why would you do that?"

She shook her head franticly. "I didn't. You must believe me, Reece. I would not do such a thing. Not even when we first met and you were so hostile toward me. And certainly not now we are betrothed."

"Ah, so the editor simply intuitively knew what I look like and decided to create his own likeness to include with your story." He stabbed the offending picture. "I recognize your work, Chelsea."

"It is my work," she said sadly, staring at the floor beneath her feet. "I cannot fathom how it came into their hands unless the page became accidently stuck with one of the others I sent."

He eyed her coldly. "A likely cover up. You are impulsive and scatter-brained, and whether you intended it or not, have done irreparable damage."

"Maybe it won't be so bad," she said hastily. "Seems doubtful anyone in England who knows you would be reading this rag."

"That is beside the point," Reece said. "The damage is done and cannot be undone. Just like you and I. I cannot marry you."

"But—but—" Her words fell on dead ears as Reece stomped across the hotel lobby and out the door. Chelsea collapsed into a puddle of despair, too numb to cry as she watched her love, her life, her future, disappear right before her eyes.

REECE THREW himself into work with a vengeance. The glass for the new greenhouse arrived and he spent hours installing it single-handedly. When Blake had been here working on the structure, he'd offered to help, but right now Reece had no desire to see any of the Masons, or for that matter, anyone who had any dealings with Chelsea.

The minister had been quite taken aback when he stopped by the sacristy and canceled the wedding. He offered to counsel Reece and Chelsea, to see if reconciliation was possible, but Reece was adamant.

It was one thing to cut Chelsea from his life. And quite another to cut her from his memories. She was everywhere. The greenhouse. The river. The cabin. His bed. Hobo wasn't the only one slinking around with his head down, only lifting it whenever he thought he heard someone coming down the driveway. More often than not it was simply a trick of the wind. Like in his early days here, folks were staying away and Reece was glad.

He deliberately lost track of time. He took his weekly floral deliveries to the hotel in the wee hours before anyone was stirring and left them around the back at the kitchen entrance where they would be seen as soon as the cook came in to work in the morning. Then he headed to Yuma and the train station, making his way to the farm without venturing back through town.

It was one such day when he arrived home later than intended, for he'd started stocking up with supplies in Yuma to avoid gossipy tongues in Bullet. If enough time passed without catching sight of him, folks would no doubt move on to more timely gossip than his broken betrothal to Chelsea.

He drove directly into the barn and saw to his horse before he headed to the cabin, stopping dead in his tracks at the sight of an unfamiliar horse grazing nearby. An intruder? His shotgun was inside, but he kept a back up one in the barn and he took off there at a run, only to freeze when he heard his name called.

He whirled as a male figure moved from the deep shadows on the porch and started down the steps toward him. Reece wondered if he looked as dumbfounded as he felt. The man's gait was hesitant as he continued toward him, not stopping until they were an arm's length apart.

"Hello, Reece. Long time."

"Luke. Yes, it has been."

His brother's face, so like his own, was a study in contrasting emotions. "So you do remember."

"I do."

"It takes a considerable long time to find a man who doesn't want to be found."

"I imagine." Reece didn't know which of them moved first, but seconds later the two brothers were hugging as tightly as the day Reece had sailed off to battle, engulfed in the silence of a past gone but not forgotten.

CHAPTER 11

Ushering Luke inside, Reece dragged out a dusty bottle of whiskey and two glasses, pouring them each a healthy measure. They clinked glasses and each took a sip. Reece was conscious of Luke taking in his simple surroundings, so different from the estate where they grew up, where Luke now lived with his family.

"It's good to see you," Reece said finally, breaking a silence that weighed heavily in the room.

"You, too. It was a rough time after we were told you had been killed in action. We waited for them to ship your body home and were eventually told it wasn't recoverable. That's when—" he shrugged.

"You did the right thing," Reece said softly.

"It doesn't feel that way." Luke rose and stuffed his hands into the pockets of his expensively tailored trousers which looked totally out of place here in the West.

"Years later we were told there 'may' have been a mistake. That it was possible you were still alive with no memory of your life before the battle."

"That part is true," Reece said. "It was several years

before my memory started to come back piecemeal, and years more before I made my way back."

"So you did come back. I felt that you might have. I sensed your presence one day, when I was out for a picnic with the family."

Reece shrugged. "You and Ann had gotten on with your lives. It was time I did the same. Not disrupt yours."

"You're the true heir," Luke said. "I'm just a stand-in. A fraud."

"Is that why you've been looking for me?"

Luke barked out a laugh. "Believe it or not, I was looking for conclusive evidence that you were, in fact, dead. So I could hold my head high. The investigator I hired got this far. He was close. I guess your friends closed ranks to protect you."

"Something like that."

"You could have knocked me over with a feather when he told me about your picture in *Lipcott's*. I was already in the Americas, following a different lead on the other side of the country. I got here as quickly as I could."

Reece nodded. "I wondered how you showed up so soon." He twirled his glass on the tabletop, then looked up at his brother. "How's Ann? The family?"

"Ann's fine. We have four children, two boys and two girls." He laughed. "An heir and a spare, just like our own parents."

Reece nodded. "Doing things the right way."

"You should come home," Luke said. "Take your rightful place."

Reece shook his head. "It's no longer my place. This is home. I spent a lot of time trying to deny my past, or escape it. Seeing you lets me know there is no such thing. But I can rewrite the future. This is where I belong. This is who I am."

"Is there a woman?"

"There is," Reece said.

Luke looked relieved. "I wondered. Ann—"

"Ann and I were never a love match," Reece said.

"She's a good wife. A good mother and hostess."

Looking at Luke, Reece suddenly felt sorry for his younger brother. There'd been no talk of love. No hint of passion. Only duty. Doing what was expected. A life from which he narrowly escaped. A life that would never suit the man he was today.

Chelsea's image swam before him. She'd said it was an accident, his likeness being included with the sketches she provided to *Lipcott's*, and furious as he had been at the time, he believed her. Yet in some roundabout way she had done him a huge service. The blunder brought Luke here, and gave Reece clarity as to what the rest of his life looked like. A life with Chelsea.

"Sit down brother, before you wear out the floor. I'll tell you what I've been up to and you fill me in on life back home. Who knows when we'll get the chance again where it's just the two of us."

WORD GOT out about Chelsea's success with *Lipcott's*, which turned her into some sort of celebrity around town. People who had avoided her earlier now rallied to share their stories, giving her more than enough material for a series of essays about life in the West. Which she intended to write. One day.

For now, people clamored to have her capture their likeness, them and their families, sometimes to display in their homes, but more often to send back to those they'd left behind in the old country. Many of them still hadn't mastered the craft of writing, at least not well enough to send letters home, but it seemed a picture really was worth a thousand words.

Chelsea did it happily, in many cases refusing payment when she knew a family's funds were in short supply. People insisted on paying what they could, and the hotel's cook was grateful when Chelsea contributed a ready supply of fresh eggs and honey to the kitchen. She knew Reece was still delivering flowers and fresh fruits and vegetables, but that he was doing it in early morning so as to avoid seeing anyone.

Knowing that, she had risen early several days in a row and gone out to the hotel's rear garden from which she had a clear sightline to the kitchen's back entrance. She managed to catch sight of him one day, which brought tears to her eyes and a pang to her heart; but at least he appeared to be well. Not suffering from a broken heart the way she was.

She couldn't remain at the hotel indefinitely, especially knowing he visited the property every week. Moving to the ranch house at the Copper Moon was one option, but she feared that being surrounded by the Masons, one big happy family, would only add to her melancholy. She'd been thrilled to learn Henrietta was in a family way at long last, and reluctantly agreed to stay until after the baby was born. After which—she might as well toss a coin as to where she ventured next. All she knew was she couldn't stay here forever. No more than she could return home.

She was still unsure of her future the day she stopped by the minister's home next door to the church to deliver the finished sketches of his family. She had created several and he had chosen one to be enlarged and framed for their front entrance hall.

"Do you mind waiting here a minute?" he asked. "I'll just fetch a hammer and nail. I could use your artistic eye to help me with the placement."

"Very well." Restlessly, Chelsea moved about the entrance hall, which was furnished simply, but clean and neatly kept. Pegs near the door held an array of hats, cloaks and jackets, while a row of rubber boots were lined up below, a few simple things that told her much about the family who lived here.

The clock chimed, startling her from her wool-gathering. What was taking the minister so long? A few more minutes passed and she had just decided to leave, moving to the front door and reaching for the handle when it turned under her fingers and the door swung open.

Reece stood on the other side. Her mouth opened but no words came out. She tried again.

"Sorry," she said. "The minister will be back in a moment. I was just leaving." She tried to brush past him, unable to see her way for the sudden wash of tears blurring her vision. Finding herself this close to Reece hurt so much, it was akin to blinding physical pain.

Reece's hand, gentle on her arm, stopped her. "I asked the minister to let me know when you were expected here."

She blinked to clear her vision. "Why?"

"I've spent several sessions with him. Recounting everything I did wrong and praying for a way to make things right."

"Things?"

"Things between us." He raised his hand and gently traced the contours of her cheek and jaw. She felt his fingers tremble against her skin. A tingling sensation radiated outward and zig-zagged its way from her head to her toes.

She couldn't rip her gaze from his. "Can you still read my expression?"

He nodded.

"Then please don't do this. Don't toy with my emotions. The invisible wounds are far from healed."

"I'm sorry if I caused you pain," Reece said. "I once accused you of being headstrong, but I am equally guilty."

"What's done is done," she said sadly. "If I could take it back, I would, but alas, it's too late to withdraw your likeness from that wretched periodical."

"Would you believe me if I told you that inadvertent bumble turned out to be most fortuitous?"

"Thank you for trying to make me feel better, but it's a wasted effort. Nothing will ever erase the regret I feel about revealing your presence to the world. I know how important your anonymity was. You trusted me with your secret and even though it was not deliberate, I forsook that trust."

"Turns out I was wrong, attempting to hide from my past."

"You were simply doing what you had to do for the sake of others."

He pulled her to him. "And hurting them in the bargain, the same way I hurt you. A fact I deeply regret."

She couldn't believe she was in his arms. A place so right and so wrong at the same time. So bittersweet. She glanced up at him, awash with unasked questions. She hoped he could still read her thoughts, because speech seemed impossible.

"My brother came to see me. All is well between us and he is relieved to know that, not only am I alive and well, but

I'm happy here, with no intention to return and claim my place on the estate."

"I see."

"It was thanks to you and that image of me in *Lipcott's* that he learned where I was. Our reunion had a most happy outcome, I might add. I never stopped to think how guilty he might feel about stepping into my life, all the while wondering if I was dead or alive. Wondering if I might show up one day and claim what I had lost. I was happy to relieve him of that burden so he can enjoy the life he deserves."

"I appreciate you telling me this." She fell silent. If only it was as easy to put things right between the two of them. "Now I really must be off."

It seemed his brother was not the only one carrying guilt. For it was plain to see when she looked up into his eyes one last time, carving a memory to last her a lifetime, as if she could ever forget him. "Please do not worry about me. I have plans as well."

"Henrietta told me you have agreed to stay until the baby arrives."

"Yes, well—" Suddenly it felt urgent she leave sooner. Leave the Masons to Reece. Leave Bullet to Reece. Move forward before she inadvertently blundered somewhere she had no business being and caused more havoc.

"Might I entice you to stay longer?"

"Longer?"

"Forever, my love. I'm intent on creating a new future. But only if it includes you."

She must have misheard. Surely—

He kissed her. Not once but three times, while she stood wooden in his arms. She had imagined this moment, dreamt of it so often that it didn't feel real.

"I love you!"

She blinked away a sheen of moisture blurring her vision. "You never told me that before. I rather thought I bullied and badgered you into a situation you fled from at the first opportunity. I mean, you never actually asked me to marry you."

He dropped to one knee, keeping hold of both her hands in one of his. "A decided oversight on my part. Chelsea Diaz, will you be my wife, to have and to hold until death do us part?"

Chelsea felt as if the heavens suddenly opened up and showered happiness on the two of them. She was too overwhelmed to respond, just stared at him in disbelief with tears spilling down her cheeks.

He gave her hands a little shake. "I've never proposed before, but I believe this is where you give me your answer."

Behind her, she heard the minister clear his throat. "For heaven's sake, miss, answer the poor man and put him out of his misery. I know for a fact this wood floor is hard on the knees."

Her tears cleared. "Yes, yes, a thousand times yes, my love."

Reece stood and gathered her against him. "That's a relief. I was starting to think I'd done it wrong."

"Impossible, my love. For I love you too. More than life itself."

Reece turned to the minister. "How soon can we arrange the marriage? My brother is here and I would dearly love to have him stand up with me."

"Mercy, yes," Chelsea said. "We need to have the wedding soon so Henrietta can be my matron of honor before she is too large with child."

"A fortnight to read the bans," the minister said.

Reece looked at Chelsea. "Is that agreeable with you?"

She melted into his embrace. "The sooner the better, to spend the rest of our lives together."

Behind them, she was aware the minister disappeared, tactfully giving them some privacy. But not nearly enough for what she had in mind.

"Is your brother staying with you?"

"He is."

"Do you think Henrietta would be scandalized if I sneak you into my room?"

"I think, where you are concerned, your cousin should be shock-proof by now."

"I say we go find out."

Two Weeks Later…

CHELSEA SMILED at Henrietta over the fabulous and fragrant bouquet Reece had created to commemorate this special day. Their wedding day. Henrietta carried a bouquet with all the same flowers in a smaller version.

"I can barely lift this," Chelsea said as Amanda, the church pianist, began to play the opening bars of "Bridal Chorus".

"It's apparent Reece knows no limits where you are concerned."

"Aren't I lucky?"

As Henrietta began her slow procession toward the altar, Chelsea counted her cousin's steps under her breath, feeling unusually calm and serene as she awaited her turn to step toward her new life. She could see Reece waiting next to his brother, Luke, eyes only for her.

"Come on, Hobo, it's our turn," she told the dog who

stood obediently at her side, a fancy nosegay on his collar with their wedding rings fastened securely beneath.

After all, it had been Hobo who brought them together.

Thank you for reading *Chelsea's Choice*. You might not know how important reader reviews are but they mean a lot. Even a sentence of two telling others you enjoyed it goes a long way with a new reader.

If you enjoyed reading it, please tell others by leaving a review wherever you purchased *Chelsea's Choice* or on Goodreads or BookBub.

If you haven't already done so, check out the other wonderful books in The Reclusive Man series.

If you'd like to read more about Laura and Storm and the entire Mason family in Bullet, keep reading for an excerpt from *Brody's Bride*, book 1 of *Seven Brides for Seven Brothers*, a classic second chance romance.

Dear Reader,

The American West in the last half of the nineteenth century offers my heroines a chance to assert their independence and also introduce them to a hero who is their match in every way. My characters have their own ideas of right and wrong, good versus evil, and deal with it on their terms. It wasn't called the Wild West for nothing. Life was about conquest, survival and persistence,

I love writing a historical genre where the reader, by the simple act of picking up the book, instantly suspends disbelief. She easily forgets about her world and her woes in a tale where no one needs to empty the dishwasher or take out the trash, and adventure lies around every corner.

As an author, it's fun to carry her away to a time and place where anything could, and often did, happen. The customs of the day and the manner of dress might be different from today's world, but people are still people. They laugh, love, hurt and heal. Celebrate and mourn. They live life large. And in the untamed wildness of the settling of the west anything can happen.

Read on for a preview of *Brody's Bride.*

Sincerely,
Kathleen

BRODY'S BRIDE - EXCERPT

A week passed during which Brody never left the ranch, using a multitude of excuses to himself to stick close. Never far from mind was the ridiculous task he'd been set. What did he know about wooing a woman? Unsuccessfully, he tried to stop his mind from going down that dark pathway to the last time he saw Laura.

Or the first.

He'd known right from the get-go that she was above his station, but his ego got the better of him. Made sure she was intrigued by his eighteen-year-old swagger and confidence.

Up until that day, anytime his thoughts strayed toward the fairer sex he pulled to mind his ma running off and leaving him, choosing her fancy snake oil salesman over him. He had thought he was past it when he met Laura. Everything about her made him feel good.

Much as he tried to deny it, those magical times with Laura had never completely left that special place carved in his heart. Even though a part of him had died the day she out-and-out rejected him in front of what felt like the entire town of Yuma, he couldn't manage to forget her. Her touch. Her scent. Her taste.

He heaved a sigh. Maybe this little exercise, to woo the schoolmarm, would shake off those cobwebbed memories once and for all.

Brody took his time getting ready. Shaved, slicked down his hair, put on his best shirt and polished his boots.

Without a word to anyone he saddled up Phoenix and made his way to Bullet.

The schoolhouse stood off to one side, shiny as a new pin, next to a field where the kids could run around and play.

He tilted back his head and studied the exterior of the building. It looked nicer than the one in Yuma. Cleaner too. Red brick must have cost Hawkes a fortune, but the man surely did like to flaunt his wealth.

Slowly Brody dismounted and tied Phoenix to the hitching post out front. Feeling like he was facing his executioner, he made his way up two steps to the front door, only to find it locked tight.

His heart lightened, feeling a reprieve. His steps were lighter, too, as he made his way back to his horse. He'd barely touched the reins, when he heard a female voice behind him.

"Brody. Brody is that you?"

Slowly he turned. Laura stood before him like a vision from the past, one he wasn't sure was real or imagined. All the pain and confusion from ten years ago rushed through him, filling his head with so much chatter he couldn't hear a thing.

Brody rocked back and forth from his heels to his toes. This little ruse of his had been a stupid idea from the get-go.

He should leave Laura to deal with Hawkes.

But he couldn't.

Hawkes destroyed everything in his path. He couldn't let the man destroy Laura. He had to get her out of there.

His head demanded he leave.

His heart propelled him to her side.

"Tell me straight. Why'd you come back here?" He

clenched his fists at his sides to keep from reaching out, from taking her in his arms."

"It's not what you think, Brody." Again, that look he remembered well, as if she was peeling back his skin and looking straight inside him. His heart beat faster. His chest felt tight.

Once upon a time he thought he knew her. Now he had no idea if he ever had. His gut clenched. He wouldn't be making that mistake again.

"You have no idea what I think."

Order *Brody's Bride* today or keep reading to see more books by Kathleen.

ALSO BY KATHLEEN LAWLESS

Western Historical Romance

Grace's Folly

Anora's Pride

Callie's Honor

Maddy's Fugitive

Widows, Babies and Brides - Box Set of the 4 Books

Sweet Western Historical Romance

SEVEN BRIDES FOR SEVEN BROTHERS SERIES

Brody's Bride - Book 1

Bradley's Bride - Book 2

Braydon's Bride - Book 3

Blake's Bride - Book 4

Bishop's Bride - Book 5

Barron's Bride - Book 6

Benjamin's Bride - Book 7

Seven Brides for Seven Brothers Box Set 1 - Prequel & Books 1 to 3

Seven Brides for Seven Brothers Box Set 2 - Books 4 to 7

Sweet Western Historical Romance

WIDOWS OF THE WILD WEST

Hope

Janie

Sweet Western Historical Romance

MAIL ORDER BRIDES

Mail Order Olivia

Mail Order Rachel

Mail Order Martina

A Bride for Shane

A Bride for Riley

A Bride for Weston

Mail Order Noelle

Chelsea's Choice

Here Come the Brides - Volume 1

Here Come the Brides - Volume 2

Sweet Contemporary Romance

Baxter

Blue Sky Island

One Cinderella Spring

One Stolen Summer

One Fantasy Fall

One Wondrous Winter

Sweet Christmas Romance Novellas

Holly's Wish

No Groom at the Inn

Steamy Historical Romance

Taboo

Unmasked

Steamy Contemporary Romance

SECRET SEDUCTIONS

Her Untamed Cowboy - Book 1

Her Undercover Cowboy - Book 2

Her Unwilling Cowboy - Book 3

Who Needs a Cowboy! - Book 4

Intimate Strangers

Women's Fiction

Fabulous at Fifty

Romantic Suspense

Final Heat

Afterburn

For a complete book list visit KathleenLawless.com

To be the first to hear about Kathleen's new releases, special fan pricing sales, and also receive a free book, sign up for her VIP Reader Newsletter at http://eepurl.com/bVosb1

ABOUT THE AUTHOR

USA Today Bestselling Author, Kathleen Lawless, blames a misspent youth watching Rawhide, Maverick and Bonanza for her fascination with cowboys, which doesn't stop her from creating a wide variety of interests and occupations for her many alpha male heroes.

With nearly 50 published novels to her credit, she enjoys pushing the boundaries of traditional romance into historical romance, contemporary romance, romantic suspense and women's fiction.

She makes her home in the Pacific Northwest and loves to hear from her readers.

Sign up for Kathleen's VIP Reader Newsletter to receive updates, special giveaways and fan-priced offers. http://eepurl.com/bVosb1

KathleenLawless.com

- goodreads.com/kathleenlawless
- bookbub.com/authors/kathleen-lawless
- facebook.com/kathleenlawlessnovels
- instagram.com/kathleenflawless
- tiktok.com/@kathleenflawless

www.ingramcontent.com/pod-product-compliance
Lightning Source LLC
Chambersburg PA
CBHW022036170626
46808CB00003B/1228

* 9 7 8 1 9 8 9 8 7 3 4 3 4 *